DATE DUE			
Sept 7	9-11-61	Jan 23	
Sept 2	10-26-61	Nov 26	
9/19/60	11-17-61	3/8	
9/20/60	15-12-61	3/29	
9/27/60	2/29/61	10/26	
10/4/60	1/2/62		
10-21-60	1/9/62	Nov 3	
11/6/60	2/9/62	0/1/62	
12-8-15	3/2/62	19	
12/16/60	4-20-62	D10	
1/20/61	5-14-62	MAR 11 '77	
3/29/61	10-18-62	APR 11 '77	
4/12/61	10-26-62		
4/14/61	10-29		
5/3/61	11-15		
4-20-61	11/20/62		
4/21/61	1-3+63		
5/4/61	5/8/63		
5/22/61	Sept 24		

170 IDEAL　　　　　　　　PRINTED IN U.S.A.

JENNIFER

By the same author

PRINCESS IN DENIM

THE HIGH WHITE WALL

ALMOST APRIL

JENNIFER

By

ZOA SHERBURNE

WILLIAM MORROW AND COMPANY
New York, 1959

To all my sons:
Herbert, Thomas, Philip, and Robert

Chapter One

JENNIFER walked home slowly, her feet shuffling through the leaves that were scattered along the walk, her eyes newly enchanted by the russet and green and gold of the October day. It wasn't even cold, not the way she remembered the late fall days in the East. There the cold had been her enemy, biting through her clothes and soaking into her bones. She had hated it, and she had hated the crowded second-story apartment, the noise from the streets, the exhaust fumes of thousands of cars, and the neon lights from a corner tavern that had blinked balefully day and night. Even in her sleep Jenny hadn't been able to escape that neon light; her dreams had been colored by it.

She walked a little faster, as if she could hurry away from the memories that she found so disturbing. A couple of girls, walking slowly toward her down the leaf-strewn street, were watching her with little half-smiles of recognition. Jennifer knew, vaguely, that they were in one of her classes at school and that they would probably expect her to stop and say something. But friendly gestures of any kind were still difficult for her; instead, she dug into the pocket of her jacket for a slip of paper and pretended to be reading an address or something as the girls brushed past her without speaking.

Almost as soon as the moment was gone she wanted passionately to recall it. This time she would be the one to break the silence. "Isn't this a glorious day?" she would say. "I can't seem to get used to this mild climate, but I *love* Washington. I'm new here; we just moved from the East at the beginning of the school year."

She knew the way the girls would look at her—surprised, but glad that she had decided to be friends.

She could say something nice about the school, too. "I've never seen such beautiful school grounds," she would tell them with perfect honesty. "Back home we were lucky to have a blocked-off street for our recess periods."

But "back home" suggested that she was just a visitor. She would have to clear up that point. She certainly wasn't a visitor. She was going to live right here in this town for always—forever.

The girls were far down the block now. Jennifer

looked after them wistfully as a scrap of laughter floated back to her. If one of them would just look back she would wave. She *would* be friendly; from now on she'd make every effort to be friends. "The way to *have* friends is to *be* one." She remembered this sage philosophy from her reading and knew that it pinpointed her trouble with deadly accuracy.

The walk seemed lonelier than ever as she crossed another street. If Molly were here, she found herself thinking, I wouldn't have to walk alone.

Even after all these years she had not stopped missing Molly. She and Molly were twins. Identical twins! They had often heard the words as they played on the grass in Central Park, or wandered hand in hand at the zoo, or walked along the street toward the school they had attended for two years.

"Why, you're identical twins, aren't you?" People always sounded so interested when they said it, teachers and bus drivers and shopkeepers and the other children. A lot of times they were teased about it, good-natured, foolish teasing. "Don't you ever forget which one you are? I should think you'd have to wear little buttons that say Molly and Jenny."

But being a twin was special. It set them apart and it meant that neither of them was ever really alone, because they were both part of another person— two halves of one whole.

They had been just eight when Molly died. Jenny remembered everything that had happened, even after all these years. A car careening around the corner, too fast, a light that was just turning red, and then Molly's body catapulting through the air and the scream that Jenny could still hear in her nightmares. The doctors assured them afterwards that in spite of the dreadful scream Molly had not known what happened. Molly hadn't even seen the car that struck her. She had run ahead of her mother and Jenny, looking back over her shoulder to see if Jenny was going to give chase. Just as she stepped off the curb her mother saw the car and screamed "Molly!" in a terrified voice. It was too late! She didn't even have time to look around and face the danger.

Jenny glanced up at the blue sky. The sun was shining, a pale sun, but sun nevertheless. It was as if summer were trying desperately to hold fast to her reign for one more day, one more golden hour.

"We're having a real Indian summer." Jennifer had heard the remark dropped casually today in the midst of the lunchtime chatter and she had liked the sound of it. She savored the phrase again, her lips smiling around the words. Indian summer—last blooming.

A leaf that had been holding perilously to the naked branch of a tree fluttered past Jenny's face and then was caught by a gust of wind and whirled away. Like a ballet dancer, Jenny thought dreamily, a ballet dancer doing leaps and turns in mid-air.

She turned into the long quiet street that led home. Edgewood Drive, the avenue sign proclaimed. Edgewood Park, the development was called in the real estate ads. It wasn't really a park at all. It wasn't even one of the new developments that had mushroomed up during the past few years. The trees that marched along the boulevard and grew on the lawns of the houses were old trees, years and years old.

That was one of the things that Jenny's father had especially liked about the place.

"You'll love the house, Nan," he had written to her mother. "Six big rooms on one floor. Everything shining and newly decorated. There's a big yard in the back and the former owner has agreed to leave the lawn mower. Can you imagine me pushing a lawn mower?" Jenny and her mother had smiled when they read that part of the letter, because it *was* hard to visualize her father pushing a lawn mower or doing any of the chores around a real house. They had always lived in apartments. "There's a big tree out in front," the letter had gone on. "Must have been there long before the house was built. Imagine us with our own tree! Jennifer's boy friends will probably carve their initials in the bark and some day we might even have grandchildren who'll want us to put up a swing."

Jenny had been amused at her father for being so excited about a tree. "What's so special about a tree?" she demanded. "You can walk through Central Park and see hundreds of them."

Jennifer still remembered the quick warm smile her mother had given her. "I think I can understand, Jenny. I think I know how he feels. A tree has roots that go down and hold fast to the earth, and we've never had roots, Jenny, never until now. It will be wonderful to have a big old tree of our own. It's so permanent."

Then Jenny's mother had gone back to reading the letter. "Hurry and get the apartment rented and all the furniture disposed of. Give the stuff away if you have to. I miss both of you very much. You'll be crazy about this town, small enough to be friendly and big enough to be prosperous. The neighbors have been dropping around already and are looking forward to meeting my two girls."

All of his letters had been like that—gay and breezy but with a warm little undertone that made them seem almost like talking to Father, almost like being able to reach across the table and touch him. And the letters always ended the same way:

"Love to you both. Jenny dear, take care of my

best girl. And Nan. . . ." And then there was always
something personal for her mother. Jenny never read
the last part of the letters.

Take care of my best girl.

Whenever she came to that part of the letter, Jennifer felt as though she were hearing her father's voice
again. "Jenny, you *will* take care of her." It hadn't
even been a question, just an urgent whisper in that
brief moment when he leaned over to kiss her good-by.
She had looked up at him and smiled and knew that
he understood.

Her mother hadn't even noticed. She was dabbing
at her eyes with fingers that were only slightly unsteady. "I'm sorry, Chuck," she said. "I don't know
why I'm acting as if you were deserting us forever.
After all, you're just going on ahead to get settled in
your new job and find us a house." Then she gave
both her husband and daughter her old dazzling
smile. "Isn't this the silliest thing?"

"I don't think it's silly," her husband said instantly.
"Why don't I just wire old Thompson that I'll be
delayed for a few days? We'll get squared away here
and all take the plane together, next week sometime.
We can live in a motel while we're house hunting.
You'd like to pick out your own home, wouldn't you?
After all, we'll be living in it for the next forty or fifty
years."

But Jenny's mother was shaking her head. "No, darling, you can't do that. You asked for this transfer. It wouldn't be fair to all those thousands of Boeing employees if you didn't report on schedule."

Jenny's father grinned at that. "They could struggle along for another week. They've managed to keep the plant going without me for this long."

"It's all settled," Jenny's mother repeated, more firmly this time. "Jenny and I will be coming before you've even had a chance to miss us. And you aren't to worry, do you hear? We'll manage beautifully."

Still he had hesitated, his dark eyes troubled and unspeakably tender. "You know how to get in touch with me, Nan. In case—in case you need me for anything."

"Of course. I'm to call Mr. Thompson, collect, and he'll get word to you. Only we won't need you, except that we'll always need you, darling."

It had been three weeks before affairs were settled and Jennifer and her mother could fly out to join him. Jennifer had been afraid that they might be difficult days, but they were surprisingly pleasant. She and her mother were together every possible moment. Sometimes Jennifer wondered if her father would have allowed them to stay behind if she had been going to school every day, leaving her mother in the loneliness of the empty apartment. But it was summer, the middle of a long hot summer.

Afterwards, when Jenny had time to think about it, she realized that her mother had worked hard at making the waiting period easier.

"Jenny dear, it's going to be another scorcher," she would say, early in the morning. "Let's make some sandwiches and go to the zoo today. You can wear shorts under your skirt and then we can lie on the grass and get a good sun tan."

Another time she said, "Why don't you sleep in the other twin bed in my room, Jennifer? That way we can keep each other company and only muss up one of the bedrooms."

Jenny was glad to move into her father's vacated twin bed. It meant that she could waken in the night and listen to her mother's gentle breathing. She could be with her and watch over her and take care of her.

It was August and oppressively hot in the small apartment. During the evenings they took walks about the steaming city, long unplanned walks that led them into queer little sections that they hadn't known existed. They always chose well-lighted streets, though, and made careful detours around cocktail bars and taverns. Jenny couldn't help worrying about what might happen if her mother ran into one of her old friends during these evening strolls, one of the friends who used to show up with such regularity when they lived in the apartment on the other side of town. Sometimes, when the doorbell rang at odd hours, Jennifer had to force herself to open the door. She was almost breathlessly relieved when the caller was someone answering the ad about the furniture or wanting to see about taking over the lease on the apartment.

One night they came in quite late to find the telephone shrilling in the empty apartment. It was Jennifer's father calling long-distance, and when the operator finally put the call through, Jenny was shocked by his anxiety, his impatience. "Jenny, I've been trying to reach you for two hours! Where on earth *were* you? And your mother? Where is she, Jenny? She's all right, isn't she?"

"We're both fine, Dad. We just went for a walk. Here's Mother now."

That was the night when he first told them about the house he had found. "I spent the first few days looking around in Seattle, but it's so big and I thought a small town would be more fun. It's such a pretty town, Nan. You'll love it."

"What about the school for Jenny?" her mother asked. "Did you find out about that?"

"Of course. There's a wonderful school within easy

walking distance. The best thing about it is that we can head in one direction and drive to the beach, or go the other way and wind up on the lake shore. I'm writing you tonight and I'll put in the floor plan of our house and the room sizes." Jenny's mother was holding the phone so that they could both hear. They smiled at one another when he said, "And listen, what do you think? There's a great big tree in our front yard."

Jenny's mother said, "That's wonderful, dear. It sounds just perfect. And don't worry about us. We're getting along beautifully."

After she had hung up, Jennifer's mother paced the apartment for a long time, walking back and forth, back and forth, with quick impatient steps. Jenny sat curled up in a corner of a big chair, trying hard to concentrate on a radio program and stifle the fear that crowded her throat and interfered with her breathing.

Finally her mother went over to the window and stood looking down into the street. The flashing neon lights made her face look haggard, and then soft, then haggard again as the colors changed. She stood so quietly that she might have been asleep, only her fingers were alive, drumming nervously against the sill.

Jenny's own fingers were clutched together until they ached, but she managed to speak in a normal, cheerful voice. "Won't it be wonderful when we get out there, Mother? When it gets hot like this we can jump into the car and drive down to the beach, maybe even go for a swim. How about that!"

Her mother didn't move or turn her head. Maybe she hadn't even heard, but her fingers were quiet. Jennifer took a quick breath and tried again. "I wonder what kind of tree we have in the front yard. Father didn't say, did he?"

Her mother turned her head then, and the smile she gave Jenny was a twisted smile. "Don't try so hard, darling. I'm all right, honestly I am." She came over and put her hand on Jennifer's head and mussed her hair. "Let's go out in the kitchen and make some lemonade, with lots and lots of chipped ice." She pressed her palms against her temples and pushed the hair back roughly. "It's so *hot*, Jenny. Anyone would be restless on a night like this."

Chapter Two

JENNIFER turned into the front yard and looked up at the tree. It was lovely, the loveliest tree in the entire neighborhood. She put her hand for a moment against the rough bark and then she ran up the walk and let herself into the front hall.

"Mother." She lifted her voice and called as she tossed her jacket on the hall chair. "Mother, I'm home!"

She waited for a second, the way she always did. Sometimes her mother didn't hear her the first time and she had to call again—and again. Like the dreadful time when. . . .

"Mother? It's me—Jenny. I'm back!"

She hated the desperate note that crept unbidden into her voice. She could feel her heart begin to work with the harsh labored strokes that seemed to pound against her temples.

19

"Mother! Where are you, Mother?" She hurried through the front room and out into the kitchen. A percolator of coffee was just beginning to bubble on the low burner and, seeing it, Jenny felt a dizzying flash of relief.

But coffee—black coffee!

Fear came back again, tearing at her. She hurried into her mother's bedroom but there was no one there. No one in the bathroom either. She was just turning toward her own bedroom when she heard the familiar sound of the back screen door slamming.

Her mother came into the kitchen, her face rosy and her eyes shining. Her arms were piled high with clean laundry.

"Oh, hi, honey! I didn't hear you come in. It was such a beautiful day that I couldn't resist getting the sheets out on the line, dryer or not. I suppose your father will think I've lost my mind." Her gay voice broke off as she saw Jenny's white face. "Darling, what on earth is the matter? You aren't ill, are you?"

Jennifer shook her head and swallowed painfully. "I couldn't find you," she said. "I called and called and you didn't answer."

Her voice was choked and she could feel that her whole body was trembling. She watched the brightness leave her mother's face; helplessly she watched as pity and love tried to soften the hurt in her mother's eyes.

"Jenny dear." She put the sheets and towels on the kitchen table, very slowly and carefully as though they might break. "Jenny dear. . . ."

"I couldn't find you," Jenny repeated doggedly. "I called and called and you didn't answer. You knew it was time I was coming. Why weren't you *here?*"

Her mother gave her a strange pleading look. "There'll be a lot of times when you'll come in and I won't be here, Jenny. I'll be shopping or visiting or maybe just having a cup of coffee with one of the neighbors." She reached over and turned off the heat under the coffeepot. "Mrs. Ferris is coming over now to have a cup of coffee, as soon as she has her clothes folded down."

Jennifer went to her room and changed from her good school clothes into jeans and a checkered shirt. She went through the familiar motions numbly and she could still feel the trembling inside her, like a sickness. A button on her shirt tangled with a lock of hair and she jerked it free, not even caring that it hurt, not even knowing that it hurt. When she started to smooth her hair, the girl in the glass stared back at her with the eyes of a stranger.

She propped her elbows on the dressing table and

put her face down into her shaking hands, fighting
for composure. It was no use. She was never going
to be able to forget. She would always walk in the
shadow of her dread. Always—always!

How carefully her father had planned this move—
the new friends and the new town and the new out-
look! "We'll start all over, honey," he had said. "It'll
be a whole new life for the three of us." He had been
so sure. They had all pretended to be so sure.

Her mother most of all. "Never again, Jenny. I
promise you, darling. We won't ever have to live
through another time like this past year."

The memory of that year had left scars on all of
them. It was a memory that could still waken Jenny
in the middle of the night and touch her with clammy
fingers. For almost the entire year she had come home
day after day, hurrying home from school, never knowing whether her mother would be there or not.
And if she was home, not knowing whether she would
be gay with the feverish bright gaiety that Jennifer
dreaded even more than the sullen silences that usually
exploded into rage and tears.

If her mother was not in the apartment, Jenny was
supposed to call her father at the office, at once. One
time she had called him and explained in halting, tearful sentences that her mother was gone again, and just

as she had hung up her mother came into the apartment, gay and laughing and a little unsteady.

"Hi, sweetie! Now don't look at me like that. I just had a short one with Dottie. She's leaving for Chicago tomorrow. I couldn't very well be a wet blanket and spoil the party, could I?"

When her father burst into the apartment a scant half hour later, Jenny's mother was taking a shower and singing at the top of her lungs. She belted a robe about her and came out to greet him, her eyes dancing and her hair curling damply about her face. She kissed him and then looked from his face to Jennifer and giggled. "Now don't tell me our little policewoman reported me absent without leave again?"

Jennifer watched her father as he mumbled something about getting away from the office early. "I thought maybe we could go out for dinner and take in a movie. Just the three of us."

But her mother brushed this suggestion aside glibly. "But, sweetie, have you forgotten that Jenny has to go to school tomorrow? I've a much better idea. We'll get all dressed up and you can take me somewhere where we can dance. You can even buy me a cocktail to celebrate, because I've been such a good girl these past . . . hmmmmm. . . . Why, it must be six months!"

"Three months," Jennifer's father corrected her. "Not quite three months, Nan." Then he had taken her by the shoulders and his voice dropped to a pleading note. "Not again, darling. You promised me."

She jerked away from him and her mouth was sullen. "You don't have to act as if I were a—an alcoholic or something. After all, I can quit any time I want to. I've proved that."

"Have you, Nan? Do you really believe it? Do you expect me to believe it?"

Her eyes widened. "Of course. And then just because I want one teeny-tiny drink in six months you act as if I were a criminal." She flounced away and went in and got dressed.

Nothing more was said about going out, but all during the long evening Jennifer and her father studiously avoided looking at one another. She knew that his eyes would reflect the same sick uncertainty that she was feeling.

It always started out this way. When her father mentioned the organization that might help her, Jennifer's mother retreated into tears and insisted that he didn't love her, he was trying to get rid of her.

"Just because I went off the deep end for a little while after Molly died," she sobbed. "How could you know the way I felt? I was the one that was there and saw the car hit her. I was the one who heard her scream."

"Other women have lost a child." Jenny's father

said the words as though he was weary of having to say them again. "And you still have Jenny. You still have me."

Jennifer's mother looked at him as if she hated him. "I know the part that comes next, Chuck. I should know, I've heard the speech so often. You loved her too. My loss is no greater than yours. Only I'm not strong like you. Like those other women who have lost a child and managed to forget it after a while."

"I'm not asking you to forget it, Nan. But we can't go on like this indefinitely. It isn't fair to me—or to Jenny. And certainly not to you."

They hardly seemed to remember that Jenny was there at such times. They never considered that she had loved Molly too, that in a way her loss was greater than theirs. She and Molly had always been so close.

Molly had died when Jenny was eight. She was nine, and ten, and finally eleven before she realized that the lives of all three of them would always be shadowed, not so much by Molly's death as by what it had done to her mother.

Her mother was very ill after the funeral and for a long time she was under the doctor's care and slept only when she took one of the little white pills that were always kept carefully out of Jenny's reach. Then came the dreadful weeks when she couldn't sleep even with the little white pills. Weeks when she paced the floor until she was ready to drop with weariness, weeks during which she grew thin and haggard and wouldn't smile even at Jenny.

And then one day her mother disappeared and they didn't find her for almost a week. A horrible week!

Then Jennifer heard her father talking to the doctor on the phone and making arrangements about the sanatorium. She told herself that she was glad that her mother was safe, that she didn't really hate her. And then she would lie awake in the darkness listening to her father pace back and forth and back and forth. She would ache with pity and know that maybe she did hate her mother after all.

Her mother was in a sanatorium for several weeks, and almost daily it seemed to Jennifer that the wings of gray in her father's dark hair spread farther back, that his smile was a little more mechanical and his eyes more haggard.

Then her mother was home again, thin and wide-eyed and somehow like a frightened child, but still Mother. Jennifer hurled herself into the outstretched arms and clung tightly to the trembling shoulders.

"Jenny darling, I'm so sorry. Mother's so sorry." She said the words over and over as her hand moved across Jenny's bent head. "It will never happen again. I promise you!"

But eventually Jenny's silence got through to her, for she lifted the girl's tear-streaked face and looked into her eyes solemnly. "You believe me, don't you, Jenny? You do believe me?"

Jenny tried to nod but couldn't. "It doesn't matter, anyway," she said thickly. "You're home again. That's what matters."

There was a little moment of absolute stillness and then Jennifer's mother spoke over her shoulder to her father, who stood in the doorway watching them. "Chuck, that—that woman we talked about, from Alcoholics Anonymous. Do you suppose . . . do you suppose she'd still come to see me if I called her?"

"I'm sure she would, Nan." It was impossible to mistake the relief in his tone, the hope.

Jennifer was ashamed that she couldn't share his feelings. It won't do any good, a stubborn little inner voice insisted. In two or three months she'll meet someone on the street, or go to a party, and the whole thing will start all over again. Can't Father see that?

But apparently he couldn't.

Her mother called the woman, a Mrs. Kirby, and she came and they talked for a long, long time. After that Jenny's mother went to meetings regularly and once, soon after the move to the new place had been decided upon, she took Jenny to one of the meetings with her to meet her friends.

562

Jennifer talked to the strangers politely, she looked about her and smiled in all the right places, but inside she felt a stiff self-conscious resentment that they should all be so unembarrassed—so . . . so *casual*. She felt an urge to shout at them, to hurl cruel taunts. "How do you know you're cured?" she wanted to demand. "How can you be so sure?" She looked at the men and the women and she wondered what they were like when they were at home. They must have families too. Maybe the families believed them when they said, "It'll never happen again. I promise you. I'm cured."

Toward the end of the evening Mrs. Kirby asked Jennifer to walk to the corner drugstore with her. It was an excuse to get her alone, Jenny knew, but there was no way that she could avoid going.

"You don't think much of our organization, do you, Jenny?" Mrs. Kirby was smiling as she put the question, but she brushed aside the girl's polite protest. "No, it's all right. I can understand how you must feel, but let me tell you about some of these people, some of the people you met tonight."

Jenny didn't want to listen but she had to. She heard about Mrs. Hammond, who had five small children, and the young woman who was a newspaper reporter, and Mr. Bishop, who had deserted his family and lost one job after another until he discovered that Alcoholics Anonymous could help him.

It sounds like a bunch of case histories, Jenny thought resentfully, and then another thought followed. Her mother, her own mother, was one of these case histories.

"We don't solicit members, Jenny," Mrs. Kirby was saying. "People must recognize their need and come to us, the way your mother did. That's the first step— the most important step—and quite often the hardest. It's difficult to believe that you yourself are an alcoholic. Everyone seems to think he can stop whenever he wants to."

"But don't some of them go right back to drinking, Mrs. Kirby?" Jennifer had to ask the question.

Mrs. Kirby sighed. "I wish I could tell you that they don't, but a great many of them do slip back. Then there's nothing to do but start over. Try again and again and again, until at last they have won their battle."

"You mean you don't think *any* cases are hopeless?"

"That's exactly what I believe, Jenny, no matter how impossible it seems to you. When a person really wants to stop drinking, he can be cured."

Jenny said nothing. As they started back, Mrs. Kirby returned to the subject. "I want to tell you one more story, Jenny, about a woman named Caroline, a woman who had everything—a fine husband, a nice home, three lovely children. She drank for years, but never to excess; she would have told you she could quit any time she wanted to. It was the old, old story we've heard so many times. Her husband died, her children married and moved away, she was lonely for the first time in her life, and so she drank more and more. Finally her children didn't encourage her to visit them; it was impossible to know what condition she might be in when she arrived. She had a small pension, enough to support her comfortably, but drinking is not a cheap pastime. She started to earn money by taking baby-sitting jobs."

Mrs. Kirby was talking softly, almost as if to herself. Jenny nodded to show that she was listening.

"She was left in charge of a baby while the parents went on a week-end trip," Mrs. Kirby continued. "There was a well-stocked bar in the apartment, and when the parents returned on Monday morning they found that their child was in the city Juvenile Welfare division. A milkman had heard him crying and decided to investigate. The baby was suffering from hunger and exposure, but he was all right; he recovered in a few days' time. The parents didn't press charges against Caroline, but the realization that the child might have died, that she might have had murder to add to the sins she had committed against her children and herself, did more good than all the lectures, all the pleading, and all the tears." Mrs. Kirby stopped for a moment and then went on. "I suppose there is always one especially black moment that makes us turn and walk in the other direction."

Jennifer nodded. "I suppose so." She was thinking of the look on her mother's face when she realized that Jenny wouldn't—or couldn't—say that she believed her. "What happened to Caroline, Mrs. Kirby?"

"She was lucky enough to find people to help her. She joined this organization. That was many years ago, but Caroline never took another drink. She never will, God helping her. Her children love her and welcome her to their homes now. She has six fine grandchildren and she leads a full and happy life." Mrs. Kirby turned her head and smiled at Jennifer as they stopped before the entrance to the apartment house. "Shall I tell you who she is, my dear?"

Jennifer managed an answering smile. "You don't have to, Mrs. Kirby."

Jenny lifted her face from her hands and picked up the brush again. She could hear her mother and Mrs. Ferris talking in the kitchen, and she knew that in just a moment she'd have to go out and join them.

Maybe Mrs. Kirby was right, she thought. Maybe that really is all behind us. She remembered the hurt in her mother's eyes when she had blurted out her tearful accusation. "You knew it was time I was coming home!"

She went into the kitchen and greeted Mrs. Ferris and helped herself to a cooky. She even perched on the drainboard for a moment and tried not to notice that the wounded look was still there in her mother's blue eyes.

"Mom, I hate to take advantage of you while you have company, but I was wondering if it would be all right if I asked a couple of the girls home some night after school. I thought we might do our homework together and maybe listen to some records when we finish."

There was surprise for just a moment in her mother's eyes, and then such brightness that Jenny wanted to weep.

"Why yes, of course, Jenny. I'd love to have you invite your friends. I'll stock up on root beer and cookies and you can have the kitchen all to yourselves. The lights are better in here."

Jenny helped herself to another cooky and then moved to the door, pausing just long enough to throw a quick smile over her shoulder at her mother and Mrs. Ferris. "O.K., then. But, speaking of homework, I'd better get at mine. Nice to have seen you again, Mrs. Ferris."

She hurried into her room and closed the door softly. Her eyes filled with tears and she didn't even try to blink them away. "Mother thinks I'm ashamed of her, she does think that. She believes that's why I've never asked any of the kids to come here—because I'm ashamed of her!"

And even as Jennifer dashed the tears away, she knew that the saddest thing about it was . . . that it was true.

Chapter Three

THAT evening her mother talked about it at the dinner table. "Jennifer has made some new friends at school," she announced with studied carelessness. "She's going to invite them here to do homework. Isn't that nice?"

Her father grinned at Jennifer. "Just so they're *girl* friends. It's a little early for her to start thinking about boys."

Jennifer made a little face at him. "How you talk! It's never too early to start thinking about boys, Father. Didn't you know?"

"No one ever tells me these things," he commented sadly, and then they all laughed.

Oh, I do love them, Jennifer thought incoherently. I wish that we could always be just like this, gay and teasing each other and being glad that we're a *family*. Looking from one smiling parent to the other, she felt her heart lift in a surge of hope. It was a hope that she quelled swiftly. Later, in a few more weeks, a few more months, perhaps she would dare to feel that they were safe. Dare to believe that the new town, the new life, had worked a peculiar magic. But not now, not yet, did she dare to believe.

The next day at school Jennifer found her attention wandering around the room when she was supposed to be concentrating on her studies. Since she had committed herself to bringing a friend home she was going to have to do something about it. But how? You didn't dash up to a complete stranger and say, "How about coming home with me this afternoon? My mother makes wonderful cookies, and we have a refrigerator bulging with Coke, and all the latest record albums."

The pretty red-haired girl she had been staring at all during study period turned her head and regarded Jennifer curiously, but instead of smiling at her Jennifer dropped her eyes quickly and pretended to be very busy looking up something in a textbook.

It went on the same way all day. At lunchtime she selected her food in the school cafeteria and then took her tray to a seat over against the wall, instead of sitting near the center of one of the long tables where other students would have to sit on each side of her as well as across the table.

Some of the boys and girls brought their lunches from home. A noisy group of them were holding down a table in the middle of the lunchroom. They all tore their lunch sacks open and shared the food just as though they were on a picnic. Occasionally a few words would emerge from the hubbub. "Gail, you *dog!* That was my ham sandwich! Now I'll be stuck with peanut butter again." "Oh, look! Janey's mother gave her some more of that yummy devil's-food cake." "Anybody interested in one slightly used apple?"

Jennifer picked up her fork and started eating her lunch, but she might as well have been consuming so much sawdust.

When a girl slid into the place beside her, Jennifer looked up hopefully, but it was evident that the new girl had selected that particular place, not for sociability but for convenience. She immediately opened a book and started to read. When Jennifer asked, in the friendliest possible voice, if she would please pass the salt, she pushed the salt shaker along the table without even glancing up and just grunted when Jenny thanked her.

The afternoon passed and it was time to go home. Jennifer took a long time getting her jacket from the locker, selecting the schoolbooks she wanted to take home with her, and applying new lipstick with the aid of a blurry mirror that had been glued up inside the locker door, a legacy from the former tenant. There were only girls in this wing of the building. The talk and the giggles and the laughter swirled all about her, but none of it really touched her. No one said, "Hi, Jenny! How about a Coke at the Malt Shop before we go home?" No one asked her what she thought of the new French teacher, whom all the girls seemed to think was a living doll. No one paid any attention to her at all.

If I fell dead right here in the hall, they'd just step over me and go right on about their business, Jenny told herself bleakly. She closed her locker and picked up her books and marched down the long hall. Another girl brushed past her, murmured something polite, and then kept right on going. Jenny's "That's perfectly all right" was spoken into a vacuum.

Outside, she stood for a moment looking about her hopefully. But everyone seemed in such a hurry. Everyone but Jenny seemed to have some specific place to go to and was in a rush to get there.

Walking home along the leaf-strewn street, she knew a feeling close to despair. She was too late; the time for being friendly was past. The first few days she had been someone new and therefore interesting in a vague impersonal way. But now she was just another familiar face, a nonentity in a gray skirt and a dark blue jacket. No one even remembered her name.

"You're Jennifer, aren't you? Jennifer Martin?" For a moment Jenny was sure that she had just imagined the friendly words, but when she turned, a short girl with sparkling blue eyes and curly brown hair was walking beside her. "I'm Patsy Gordon. My aunt is Mrs. Ferris."

"Mrs. Ferris? Oh, yes, of course. The lady who lives next door. Do—do you live there too?"

"Oh, no. I live thataway." She made a vague gesture in the opposite direction. "I'm just delivering these pears to my Aunt Margaret." She looked down at the shopping bag she was carrying in one hand and shrugged. "We have a tree just loaded with the things and we all just *hate* pears. Aunt Margaret said she didn't want any to can, just some for eating." She stopped then and grinned at Jennifer. "Would you like one? To eat, I mean, now?"

"Why, yes. I'd like one very much, thank you." Jennifer shifted her books and then put her free hand into the shopping bag. "Thank you," she repeated.

"You're new, aren't you?" Patsy said, as Jennifer bit into the pear. "I haven't seen you around much."

"No one sees me," Jennifer said. "That seems to be my big trouble. I just sort of blend in with the woodwork."

The other girl looked shocked. "What a thing to

say! You don't blend in with the woodwork at all. As a matter of fact, you're kind of cute."

"I am?" Jenny was honestly amazed.

"Well, at least you don't have the kind of face that would make anyone run screaming," Patsy continued honestly. She looked at Jennifer quickly to see if she showed any signs of resentment. They both started to laugh.

Patsy had a nice laugh. You knew right away that it was the kind of laugh that would still be amused if the joke was on herself.

"That's probably the most doubtful compliment I ever heard in my life," Jenny said.

"I didn't mean for it to sound quite like *that*," Patsy said, unabashed. "But you *were* being a little stuffy. Anyway, I'm glad to see that you have a sense of humor."

"Why?" Jenny asked. "Why on earth should you care whether I have a sense of humor or not?"

Patsy gave her another quick grin. "Oh, you're supposed to be my good deed for the week."

"I am?" Jenny asked again. "Why?"

"Because Aunt Margaret thinks you're a sweet little thing who is lonely, and she has appointed me a committee of one to remedy the situation. I was going to strike up a conversation with you in the lunchroom today, but you hemmed yourself into a corner and it was impossible to get at you." All this was reported so matter-of-factly that Jenny felt her brief embarrassment ebbing away.

"It's very kind of your aunt, and of you, too. But I'm really not lonely."

Patsy squinted at her. "Would you rather I just went away and minded my own business then?"

"Oh, no, please don't!" Jenny spoke quickly and then added in confusion, as the other girl smiled, "Well, O.K., then. Maybe I am lonely—a little."

"We'll certainly have to do something about that," Patsy said briskly. "But you'll have to help too. No one wants to feel they're being snooted."

"Snooted? By me?"

"By you," Patsy said firmly, and then continued in a singsong voice. "Bayou—the outlet to a lake, or one of the delta streams of a river. Usually found in the southern United States."

But Jennifer refused to smile. "Do they really think I'm stuck-up, Patsy?"

"Well, you come from back East and your clothes are the last gasp, and your father drives you to school once in a while in that dreamy convertible, and according to school records he's some sort of big shot at Boeing. That makes you a big wheel, but even big wheels can give out with a smile once in a while, or can't they?"

The girls were in front of Jenny's house now and they stopped walking.

"Patsy . . . would you come in, just for a moment, and meet my mother? She's been worried because I haven't made any friends at school and. . . ."

"And you told her that you were going to invite some of the kids home to do homework with you, and eat cookies, and listen to records, and guzzle Cokes from the refrigerator. My dear aunt reported it all word for word. You should have heard her. 'The poor child,' she said. 'You can tell that she's just miserably lonesome, but she's trying so hard to make her mother believe that she's happy here.'" Patsy's solemn voice was belied by the twinkle in her eyes. "My heart absolutely bled for you, Jennifer Martin."

"Then you *will* come in for a little while?"

"Of course, why else would I be stalking you? You don't think I walked this far out of my way just to deliver pears, do you? And why do you think I brought my books?" She glanced toward her aunt's house and then shoved her schoolbooks at Jenny. "You can go in and break the news to your mother while I take these disgusting things to Aunt Margaret." She hurried off without another word, but Jennifer stood watching until the house next door had swallowed up her new friend.

Her friend! Of course it was a little early to know

whether they would really be friends, but she could dream, couldn't she?

She hurried into the house and tossed her jacket and all the books on the hall table. "Hi, Mother! I'm home!"

"Out here, Jenny. I'm in the kitchen."

Jennifer followed the sound of her mother's voice. She was just applying the last bit of frosting to a plate of fresh cupcakes. The kitchen still held the spicy odor of warm cake.

"Oh, yummy!" Jennifer said. "I brought company. Patsy Gordon. She's the niece of Mrs. Ferris, next door."

"Oh, yes, Margaret told me she had a niece about your age. How nice that the two of you got together."

Jennifer opened her mouth to say something, then closed it firmly. She had an idea that her mother would be happier about this new friendship if she thought that Jenny had made the opening gesture.

Patsy came up the back walk and knocked on the screen door. "My mother taught me always to come in the back way, just in case my shoes happened to be dirty. Besides, it was closer," she explained artlessly, after she had been properly introduced to Jennifer's mother.

"I'm going to leave you two for a little while," Mrs. Martin said presently. "I thought I'd walk over to the supermarket and get some fresh vegetables. Jenny, take good care of your little friend."

Jenny and Patsy smiled at each other when the door closed behind her. "Little friend! Honestly, don't parents just fracture you?" Patsy said.

Jenny did not answer. "Well," she said, "shall we study in here, where we're handy to the refrigerator and the light is good, or would you rather work in my bedroom?"

"I'd love to see your room," Patsy confessed. "I just adore snooping around other people's houses. But we might as well study here in the kitchen. Let's spread our books out so we'll look busy."

Jennifer showed her all around the house, feeling a quiet pride that everything was so orderly, that the curtains were crisp and fresh and the paint still unscarred.

Patsy read the titles of all Jenny's books and all her record albums. She admired the new bedroom furniture and the sewing cabinet that doubled as a desk.

"What a blow our house is going to be after all this," Patsy confessed. "You'll simply flip when you see the utter chaos in my bedroom. I share it with my sister Glenda. She's almost three years younger and she has all the finer instincts of a pack rat, believe me. That kid saves everything—but everything!"

Jennifer smiled, warmed by Patsy's matter-of-fact

assumption that of course she would be visiting Patsy's house, meeting Patsy's family.

They went downstairs and admired the recreation room, which wasn't quite finished yet. "Dad is going to finish it himself," Jenny reported proudly.

Patsy nodded agreeably. "Well, I just hope he isn't as slow as my father. It took him about three years to enclose the front porch for an extra sleeping room."

They were back in the kitchen arguing good-naturedly about an assignment when Patsy glanced at the kitchen clock and announced that she really had to be starting home. "I called Mother from Aunt Margaret's house and told her where I was, but I promised her I'd be home right after five."

"Well, if you gotta I guess you gotta," Jenny said. "But Dad will be along any minute. He'd be glad to drive you home, I know."

Patsy's blue eyes sparkled. "In the convertible? In that black-and-white job with all the silver plate?"

"The very same," Jenny assured her gravely. "Only us aristocrats call it chrome."

They had another Coke while they waited for Jennifer's father. Jenny put away the record player that had furnished background music all during algebra and world history, but had been silenced while the girls tried to memorize French phrases.

"It's been so much fun, Patsy," Jennifer said. "I hope you'll come again."

"All you have to do is ask me," Patsy reminded her. "Almost any of the girls would be glad to come if you asked them, don't you know that?"

"I'm going to believe it anyway, even if it isn't true," Jenny said. "From now on I'm going to be so friendly that it'll be absolutely nauseating."

"You don't have to go that far," Patsy objected. "Just try a smile here, a gentle word there. A handful of silver tossed to the peasants as you roll along in your new convertible."

"You," Jenny said pleasantly, "are absolutely nuts."

When her father turned into the driveway both girls ran out to the car. "Dad, this is my friend Patsy Gordon," Jenny said. "I told her you'd drive her home. It's only eight or ten blocks."

"Sure. Climb in." Her father slid over to make more room. "You'll have to give me some directions, though."

Patsy gave him the directions. "You just go down Edgewood to the main boulevard; there's a stop light there, you can't miss it. Then turn right for about three blocks and then left. . . ." She hesitated for a moment and then concluded in a little rush, "And then I'm home. But Mr. Martin, would you *please* put the top down?"

He grinned and pushed the button, which immediately started folding the top.

Jennifer talked all the way to the Gordon house, and after they had left Patsy and started home again she still continued to chatter.

"I think someone put a nickel in this kid and the machinery got jammed," Jenny's father complained to his wife, as he went into the house and kissed her. "She's been talking a blue streak."

But Jennifer knew that he was just kidding. Even before he gave her a smart spank and then turned, whistling, into the living room in search of his paper, she knew that he was pleased. Her feet danced as she helped set the table.

She thanked her mother again for letting her have Patsy come to visit. "The cupcakes were scrumptious. We had three apiece and two Cokes. I've never had so much fun just doing schoolwork. Patsy moved here last year, did I tell you?"

"You've never had a special girl friend before," her mother reminded her. "Not since Ruby, that girl you were so fond of when you were in about the sixth or seventh grade."

Jennifer nodded without answering, but if her mother noticed the sudden quiet she didn't comment.

Of course she remembered Ruby. The sharp-fea-

tured face framed by glossy black ringlets, the dark
eyes, and the smile that was sly rather than friendly.
Jenny had loved her with the unthinking, unreason-
able affection of the very young. Ruby was so clever,
and she was so pretty. She didn't seem to mind having Jenny trot adoringly at her heels, even though she
was older and had so many interesting friends her own
age.

It never occurred to Jenny that actually Ruby had
no friends her own age. The reason was perfectly
simple: Ruby thought only of Ruby. She tolerated
the younger girl's admiration only because she was
flattered by it. She allowed Jenny to buy her candy
bars and movie magazines and once in a while she'd
consent to go to a Saturday matinee—Jenny's treat, of
course.

It was after one of these Saturday matinees that
Jenny had coaxed Ruby to come home with her. If
she lived to be a thousand years old, Jenny thought,
she would never forget that afternoon. They let themselves into the apartment with Jenny's key and found
her mother collapsed in a heap on the kitchen floor.

"Is she dead, Jennifer, is she dead?" There had
been thrilled excitement underlying the horrified
words, but Jenny did not notice. They rolled her
mother over and Jenny ran to the bedroom for a pillow. Ruby had straightened up, her nose twitching,

her eyes unbelieving. "She isn't sick at all," she said in a flat, disappointed voice. "She's just plain *drunk*."

Jenny wanted to hit her, hard, but instead she eased the pillow under her mother's shoulders. "She's sick, Ruby. She really is sick. She . . . she hasn't had one of these attacks for a long time."

"Attacks! You mean she hasn't been on a drunk for a long time. She's dead drunk, that's what she is, and I think it's perfectly disgusting!"

"As if anyone cares what you think. As if anyone *cares*." She knew in the black rage of that moment that Ruby wasn't wonderful at all. "I think you'd better go, Ruby," she said in a shaking voice.

Ruby glared down at her furiously. "You just bet I'm going." The door slammed behind her like a cannon shot, but Jenny scarcely noticed. She was already wringing cloths out of cold water to put across her mother's forehead.

She had never told anyone about it. Ruby was someone she wanted to forget. And she *had* forgotten, until her mother's careless remark brought back the whole affair.

Jennifer went in to wash up for dinner and she could hear her father whistling as he moved about in his room getting into the comfortable short-sleeved shirt and old slacks he liked to wear around the house.

"I like your little friend," he told Jennifer, as they sat down to dinner. "Even if she *is* convertible-happy."

Jennifer grinned and thought that she must remember to repeat the phrase to Patsy—convertible-happy! She knew just the way Patsy would look at her, pretending to be furious but scarcely able to hold back the laughter.

"I feel as if I'd known Patsy for a long, long time," Jenny said. "Do you ever have that feeling about someone you've just met?"

"*En rapport*," her father said. "A French phrase meaning completely compatible. You like each other because you think and feel the same way about things. Does that make any sense to you?"

"Yes, I guess so. Anyway, I hope I'm like Patsy. She's so much fun."

Last year, when Patsy had been new, maybe someone had gone out of her way to make her feel welcome. Jenny hoped someone had. "And when another new girl comes along it'll be my turn," she vowed to herself solemnly.

Chapter Four

"MEETING new people is like learning to eat olives," Jennifer confided to Patsy at the end of the next week. "After the first three or four you begin to enjoy them."

"Well, thanks," Patsy said. "As one of the first four olives I thank you from the bottom of my heart for this priceless compliment."

Jenny giggled and shifted her books to the other arm. "Oh, you know what I mean," she said lightly.

"Do I? Well, who was the fifth olive—the one that you started to enjoy?" Patsy demanded. "It wouldn't be Griff Nolan, would it?"

"Griff . . . oh, you mean that tall, shy boy? The one with brown eyes and the cowlick and the nice smile and the blue suède shoes?"

"M-m-m. That's Griff, all right. He isn't really shy, though. He's a lot of fun when you get to know him." Patsy gave a little skip to keep up with Jennifer's long-legged stride. "Hey, slow down, will you? We aren't going to a fire!"

They were going, as a matter of fact, to Patsy's house to work on their French assignment. Patsy's mother was French. She had been born in a little town just outside Paris and had married Patsy's father during World War II. Even after being an American for all the intervening years, Patsy's mother had what her children were fond of calling her pea-soup accent.

The first time Jennifer had visited the Gordon house she was a little startled by Patsy's mother, but now she was used to her. Mrs. Gordon was small and dark and excitable. She waved her hands a lot and her voice rose several tones when she got upset about anything. Her husband called her the French Revolution, but he said the words proudly, as though he found her explosiveness a highly desirable trait.

"Don't let Mother throw you," Patsy had advised Jennifer that first day. "She yells a lot, but it doesn't really mean a thing. She just wants to make sure that we hear her."

Studying at the Gordon house was never dull. Instead of sitting at the table, they followed Mrs. Gordon around while she made pies, dampened down clothes, or even cleaned cupboards and drawers.

They spoke French, haltingly at first. But using the words gave them a little feeling of intimacy with the language. The children, the dishes, the books and pencils—they learned to incorporate the new phrases into their everyday conversation.

"It's like having a long-playing record in French," Patsy told Jennifer. "Only Mother isn't exactly predictable, is she?"

"You can say that again," Jennifer said feelingly.

"O.K. I will. It's like having a long-playing record in French. Only Mother isn't very predictable, is she?"

They both laughed and sat down at the end of the dining-room table to compare notes on the history assignment. It was when they were putting away the books and papers and Jenny was getting ready to go home that Patsy asked her, "What were you and Griff talking about in the lunchroom today? You both seemed so interested in what you were saying that I didn't have the heart to barge in."

"Oh, it wasn't important. Miss Kramer had asked how many of us had ever visited the Statue of Liberty and Griff had and so had I, and we got talking about it afterwards."

"How fascinating," Patsy drawled. "What else did you have to say to each other?"

"Nothing," Jennifer admitted. "Except he said he'd be seeing me around."

The days and weeks ran together pleasantly. Jennifer occasionally found herself singing as she worked around the house or helped her father polish the car or pushed the lawn mower. The days were crisp and cool and she had to wear a coat as she mowed the lawn, but it was still a task she loved. "Good for my waistline," she explained when her father insisted that this was a man's job. It rained so often that the grass stayed velvety green; there hadn't even been a touch of frost and it was almost November.

At school everyone was talking about Halloween parties and dances and it didn't even bother Jennifer that she hadn't been invited to one of these. There was plenty of time, years and years of time. Maybe next year *she* would give a Halloween party; she'd know almost everyone by then.

More and more often when the telephone rang it was someone for Jenny. She spent hours giggling and talking and laughing with her new friends on the phone. A girl who lived farther along the street, Elsie McNeill, usually stopped and walked to school with her. Jenny tried out for basketball and was hopeful that she might make the team. Patsy was definitely in —she would probably be the star. In spite of being so short she was amazingly good. It was fun watching her dart in and out among the other players, leaping high to throw the ball directly into the basket.

Jennifer complained bitterly about homework, just

the way the others did, but she was pleased that her marks were so good. Her father and mother would be simply delighted if she made the Honor Roll and had her name posted on the bulletin board in the school auditorium.

One evening, as she prepared a theme while listening to a TV program with one ear, she heard her father telling her mother about some big wheel who was going to be in town over the week end. Even as her mind digested this bit of information she had no idea that it would mean anything to her personally.

It was a couple of days later, when she was rummaging in the cupboard for an after-school snack, that she found the liquor bottle. It was tucked in carelessly behind a couple of cracker boxes. There had certainly been no effort made to hide it, and the seal wasn't even broken.

Jennifer replaced the cracker boxes and shut the cupboard door quickly. She got down off the kitchen stool feeling a little sick and unsteady; when she went back and tried to concentrate on her schoolwork she couldn't forget about it. The leering brown bottle with its flamboyant label and impressive seal, standing there like an evil genie, waiting to tear down all that they had rebuilt; ready to destroy all the precious things they had found in this new life.

I'll smash it, Jennifer told herself that night, after all the house was quiet. I'll go and get it out of the cupboard right now and smash it. I'll tell them I was getting some crackers and I accidentally knocked it over.

She slipped out of bed, her heart hammering against her ribs, and moved quietly across the room and out into the hallway. There wasn't a sound in the entire house except the ticking of the clock on the mantel. Once a floor board squeaked and she almost gave up the idea. What would she say if they heard her and asked her what she was doing prowling about the house in the dark?

Normally, when she got up for a midnight raid on the refrigerator, she clicked on the lights as she went. There was something sinister and dangerous about moving alone in the ghostly dark. She moved the kitchen stool as quietly as she could, and when she opened the cupboard and reached past the cracker boxes her groping hand found the bottle immediately.

Jennifer drew a sharp, hurting breath. She lifted the bottle high above her head and then dashed it to the floor, where it shattered with a crash as loud as the voice of doom.

For a second afterwards she stood frozen, listening to the sound of voices from her mother's room, the click of the night lamp being turned on, and then the staccato sound of hurried footsteps. Jennifer stepped down from the stool and a sharp stab of pain jabbed at her. Why hadn't she thought about the shattered glass? The kitchen door swung open and her father stood there staring at her. His eyes were still heavy with sleep, but there was fright in his eyes, too. It was an effort for Jennifer to speak quietly.

"Don't come in here in your bare feet," she said. "I knocked over a bottle and the floor is covered with bits of glass. I got a piece of it in my heel, I think." She was standing on one foot and the blood from her heel dripped down to add to the mess of liquor and glass on the freshly waxed linoleum.

"What on earth happened?" That was her mother. She had taken time to put on her bedroom slippers and was jamming her arms into her robe as she came along the hall. A quick look told her what had happened. She crossed swiftly to Jennifer's side and her eyes were dark with concern. "Sit down, honey, and let's have a look at that foot."

"It's all right," Jenny insisted, white-faced. "It doesn't even hurt. Just as soon as it stops bleeding a little I'll clean up this mess." Her mouth trembled. "Oh, Mother, your nice clean floor! I'm so sorry."

Her mother was dabbing at Jenny's heel with a clean handkerchief. She looked up and shook her head. "Don't worry about the floor, for pity's sake.

What about your foot? Does it feel as if there's still glass in it?"

"It doesn't feel like anything. It aches a little bit, but that's all. Serves me right for being so—so clumsy." She was staring at her mother's bent head as she spoke, but she didn't even look up. Jennifer raised her eyes slowly and saw that her father was watching her. He had gone back and got his slippers and a bottle of disinfectant from the medicine cabinet. Silently, he handed the bottle to his wife, but his eyes were asking a thousand tormented questions as they searched Jenny's.

"I started to get some crackers. I got hungry. And like a fool I didn't turn on the light so I could see what I was doing." The explanation died away on her lips as her mother dabbed at the cut with the disinfectant. In a way the pain was welcome. She closed her eyes and bit down on her lip, and when she looked at her father again he was carefully not looking at her.

"Well, it couldn't be helped. No use crying over spilled liquor, I always say." But there was a curious heaviness in her father's voice, as though he were disappointed in her.

After the wound had bled for a little while, Jenny's mother bandaged her foot and sent her back to bed. Hobbling along the hall, Jennifer looked back at her father, who was already busy with broom and dustpan sweeping up the shattered glass.

Her mother tucked her into bed and then, as an afterthought, asked if she was still interested in a snack. "I'll bring you a glass of milk and some cookies," she offered, but Jennifer shook her head.

"No, thank you, Mother. I'm not hungry any more."

Her mother went back to the kitchen and Jennifer could hear the two of them talking as they mopped up the floor and put the kitchen to rights. It seemed poetic justice that her heel was throbbing and that she felt sick at her stomach. The sweetish odor of the spilled liquor was heavy in the room; that was probably what was making her nauseated.

She slid out of bed and pushed the window up as far as it would go. It would throw off the air-conditioning system, but Jennifer really didn't care. She hopped back to bed and crawled between the covers again. She was shivering a little.

Long after her mother had peeked in to see if she was all right and then gone back to her own room, long after the house was quiet again, Jennifer was still wide awake. For some reason she couldn't forget the disappointment in her father's eyes. He knew that she'd broken the bottle on purpose. He knew! She couldn't be sure that her mother knew, but that one searching glance her father had given her told Jennifer beyond any shadow of doubt that her explanation had not satisfied him. But surely he could understand why she had done it. Even if he didn't exactly approve, he ought to be able to understand why.

But you can't destroy all the liquor in the world by smashing one bottle, she thought sadly. I guess I shouldn't have done it. She turned her head restlessly on the pillow. I don't suppose it did any good at all.

Sleep was a long time coming, and Jenny woke feeling spent and looking hollow-eyed. She insisted on going to school, though. She wore one bedroom slipper, and although her father offered to wait and drive her over she assured him that it wasn't at all necessary.

"I'll manage just fine. Elsie is coming over to walk with me. We'll take our time."

Her mother fussed a little, but was eventually won over by Jenny's arguments about missing school assignments. "But Mother, the whole system is so different out here. If I get behind in the work I'm just going to be lost, that's all."

She was glad to get out of the house. It seemed to Jennifer that the whole place still reeked of whisky.

By evening her heel was only a little stiff and sore. It was almost possible to pretend that the entire episode was something she had dreamed. The kitchen linoleum was as glossy as ever. No one said anything about the accident; no one questioned whether it had been an accident.

On Saturday forenoon, when Jennifer was enjoying her late breakfast, her mother reminded her that they were having guests that evening.

"That company executive and his wife—Antiel, their name is. Dad's taking us to the Beach Club for dinner. You'll be all right, won't you, Jenny? I thought you could ask Patsy to come over and stay with you. I'll get a couple of extra lamb chops."

"Will you be very late, do you suppose? I mean, should I ask Patsy to stay all night?"

"You can ask her if you like, but it really won't be necessary. We'll be home fairly early. It's just a dinner."

"Oh. Not . . . not a dinner dance then? Not a real party?"

Her mother looked at her, amazed. "Darling, I just told you. We're going to meet here and then drive over to the Beach Club for dinner. After that we'll drive the Antiels to their ten-thirty plane and we should be home well before midnight."

Jennifer drew a little sigh of relief. It really wasn't going to be a party then, the kind of party where some idiot would be sure to argue with her mother about having a sociable drink.

"Can I do anything to help?" Jenny asked, after she

had cleared away the breakfast dishes. "Anything special you want done?"

"I'll probably ask you to run to the store for me after a while. We're keeping everything pretty casual, but we'll need something for appetizers, and probably some potato chips and a couple of bottles of mixer." Her mother was bustling around the kitchen as she spoke. "I thought I'd wear my green sheath dress. Do you think it's too much for just a dinner?"

"People usually dress at the Beach Club, don't they?" Jenny asked heavily. "You'll look fine."

"I just hope Mrs. Antiel isn't the plunging-neckline-mink-stole type. Those women depress me." She went on chatting just as lightly as ever, as she got out her best silver and cups and the flower frog for her good vase. "I suppose you should stop at the little florist shop and get some flowers. Chrysanthemums are nice this time of the year. Yellow and brown ones."

If I could just sit and talk to her, Jenny thought half a dozen times that day. If I could just say, "Now look here, Mother. . . ." She couldn't, though. And the reason was all mixed up with the way Jennifer's father had looked at her that night she smashed the bottle.

When the house was ready for the guests, Jennifer got dressed to go to the shopping center. She put on a full skirt and a crisp pink blouse and brushed her short brown hair up and back so that it framed her face softly. Brown hair, brown eyes, stubby brown lashes. She wasn't exactly satisfied with the face that looked back at her from the mirror, but there wasn't much she could do about changing it.

She went to the shopping center and got all the things that were on the list her mother had made out. Late in the afternoon, while her mother took a nap, Jennifer sat on the front steps and watched her father as he trimmed the borders of the grass and clipped the hedge.

"I'm probably doing this all wrong," he told Jennifer cheerfully. "I just don't have green thumbs." He whistled under his breath as he worked, and frequently complained about how forty-year-old knees didn't have much bend in them. Jennifer couldn't bring herself to mention the things that both of them were trying to forget.

Her mother was arranging the chrysanthemums in a tall vase when Jennifer went into the kitchen a short time later. She looked pretty, with her eyes shining and her hair brushed forward into the becoming bangs that gave her face a pixy quality. She looked pretty and happy and at peace with the world. She had slipped on a housecoat so that she could put on her dress just before the guests arrived.

"Aren't these beautiful?" she crooned to Jenny, her face tipped forward over the shaggy flowers.

Jenny went in and sat on the side of the bed and watched as her mother slipped into the green sheath dress and then applied make-up and perfume and her best earrings. She motioned for Jenny to zip the back of her dress and then removed the bobby pins from her mouth and tucked them into her shining hair. "Well, I've put on a little weight since we've been out here, but I can still get into a size fourteen," she announced with evident satisfaction.

Jennifer was silent as her mother whirled and posed before the mirror, admiring her dress from all angles. She couldn't help remembering another evening, two or three years ago.

Then, as now, her mother had been gay as she dressed to go out for dinner with some of the company personnel.

"Mr. Griggs is an important man, Nan," Jenny's father had assured her seriously. "A lot may depend on how he likes us." Both Jenny and her mother had recognized this as a warning.

"Darling, I'll be an absolute angel!" Jennifer's mother had promised extravagantly.

Jenny didn't know what had taken place that evening. She had only heard the scene afterwards, the long, bitter quarreling that had gone on until the pale morning hours. The quarrel was resumed off and on during the next week and finally resulted in a period of cold warfare that was somehow worse than the shouting and the tears.

She was staring blankly at the pale green carpet on the bedroom floor. Her mother's voice interrupted gently. "Jenny, you aren't ill, are you? Your heel isn't bothering you again?" Her mother's hand was firm and cool against her cheek and the blue eyes looking down into hers were anxious. "You've been so quiet all afternoon. You don't feel neglected because we're going off and leaving you?"

"Of course not." Jenny spoke stiffly. And after a moment she got up and went out to sit on the porch and wait for Patsy.

Chapter Five

PATSY didn't arrive until almost time for the Antiels to be there. The two girls went into Jennifer's room to put away Patsy's pajamas and toothbrush. Patsy had brought along a new record and they played that, sitting on the edge of the bed and rocking back and forth with the music.

"I'm glad you asked me over tonight," Patsy confided, as they flipped the record to hear the other side. "I was scared to death Mrs. Phillips was going to call and ask me to baby-sit. Those two kids of hers just frazzle me. They just simply wear me to a pulp, that's all."

"But if you don't like to baby-sit for them, why do you go?" Jenny asked reasonably. "You could tell Mrs. Phillips that you're all booked up, couldn't you?"

Patsy shook her head. "Oh, no, I couldn't do that. She might find out that I didn't have another job and then she'd never ask me again."

"But you wouldn't care. You don't like to baby-sit for her anyway."

"I know." Patsy scowled thoughtfully. "But then her feelings would be hurt. She'd think I didn't like the kids or something."

"Well, do you like them?" Jenny demanded patiently.

"Of course not. I hate the little monsters!" She laughed when Jenny looked puzzled, and then went on seriously. "I know it must sound pretty confused, but I hate to hurt anyone's feelings. It's so much easier to just sort of detour around the absolute truth and leave everyone feeling relaxed and happy."

Jennifer smiled at her friend. "So I suppose you'll go on the rest of your life baby-sitting for little monsters just so their mothers won't know you think they're little monsters."

"Oh, no, not the rest of my life," Patsy interrupted happily. "Your baby-sitting career is just about washed up in this town by the time you get to be a junior in high school."

"I've never done any baby-sitting," Jennifer admitted absently. "I wouldn't know the first thing about it. Back home when people wanted a baby sitter they just picked up the telephone directory and called an agency."

"I wish you'd quit saying 'back home,'" Patsy objected. "This is your home. And what do you mean you've never done any baby-sitting? How do you earn your movie-magazine-Saturday-matinee money?"

Jenny shrugged. "I've never earned any money. Dad gives me an allowance when he thinks of it."

"What happens when he doesn't think about it?"

"Oh, I remind him," Jenny said.

A taxi pulled up in front of the house while they were still sitting in Jenny's room talking. From behind the crisscrossed curtains they watched the couple who got out and came up the walk. The doorbell rang and they heard Jennifer's father answer it and lead his guests into the living room. There was a polite, subdued murmur of voices, which grew a little more animated when Jennifer's mother joined the group.

"Maybe we won't have to go and meet them," Jennifer whispered. "Maybe we can just stay here until after they leave and then go and fix our dinner."

"But why should we want to hide?" Patsy asked incredulously. "Don't you like parties?"

"I've an idea that I won't care much for this one," Jenny said a little grimly. But when her mother came to the door and called her a few moments later, Jenny led Patsy into the living room and was polite and attentive as her mother made the introductions.

Mr. and Mrs. Antiel might have been carbon copies of a dozen other couples Jennifer remembered from the old life. Mr. Antiel was tall and well tailored and a little bald. The super-salesman type, Jennifer told herself. Before the evening was an hour older he would be calling her mother "little lady," and thinking up excuses to get Jennifer and Patsy out of the room so that he could start telling stories. Mr. Antiel undoubtedly thought of himself as a genial, hard-drinking, back-thumping, and most attractive fellow. It would probably hurt his feelings if he knew that Jennifer disliked him on sight.

His wife was a type, too. Jennifer's mother hadn't been far wrong in her plunging-neckline-mink-stole summary. Except that in this case it was a short fox cape that topped the sophisticated black dinner dress. Mrs. Antiel insisted that all of them must call her Faye.

"She certainly has a gorgeous figure, hasn't she?" Patsy whispered, when the two girls were in the kitchen getting more potato chips and salted nuts.

"Too thin," Jennifer said shortly. "I mean, you can tell it's the kind of figure she has to work at."

"How can you tell?"

Jennifer scowled at the bowl of potato chips in her hands. "Just watch her. She won't touch any of this junk, but she'll have three or four drinks, one right after another. Then at dinner tonight she'll just push the food around on her plate."

"If I had a figure like that I wouldn't care about food," Patsy declared, and bit into a potato chip dreamily.

Jennifer's father came into the kitchen at that moment and started assembling things for the drinks. He got the bottles of mixer and a tray of ice cubes and the tall glasses from the top shelf. "I'll put some Coke and ice into these frosted glasses for you two kids," he said cheerfully over his shoulder, and reached into the cracker cupboard for a bottle of liquor, a twin to the bottle Jennifer had smashed a few days earlier.

The girls took the nuts and potato chips and cheese crackers into the living room. Jennifer's mother thanked them with a bright smile as they put the bowls down on the coffee table.

The telephone rang and Jenny went to answer it, just as her father came in from the kitchen with a tray. "Here we are," she heard him saying as he moved past her into the living room. "You wanted plain bourbon and water. Is that right, Faye? And yours was soda, Dave. Nan?"

Jennifer was listening so hard that she forgot to say hello when she lifted the receiver. After a moment a girl's voice asked rather plaintively if this was the Martin home. It was one of the girls from school, just wanting to talk. Jennifer explained that they had company and said she'd call back. When she went back into the living room, her father had a glass in his hand and was smiling at everyone. "Well, cheers!" he said abruptly, and almost at once glanced at his watch.

Jennifer went out into the kitchen to get the glasses for Patsy and herself. When she came back, the men were sitting side by side on the davenport talking business and the women were chatting about clothes.

Faye's glass was emptied quickly and Jennifer's father hastened to refill it. "How about you, Dave?" he asked, pausing for a second in the doorway. "We've just about time for one more round." Dave grunted assent and finished his drink, but Jennifer's mother shook her head when her husband glanced at her.

"I'll just nurse this one along, I think."

Her glass was beside the bowls on the coffee table, and it was still more than half full. If I just happened to bump it with my elbow, accidentally of course . . . Jennifer found herself thinking. But as she moved a step closer her mother reached out and took the glass.

"Steady there," she said in tones of deep amusement. "I don't trust you after that business of the other night."

Jennifer's eyes were startled, but her mother wasn't even watching her. She was already telling Mrs. Antiel about the accident.

"We had a little excitement a few evenings ago," she was saying so easily that Jennifer knew she didn't even suspect that the bottle might have been broken purposely. Her first feeling of relief was replaced by irritation. She had accomplished nothing at all.

"Well, little lady," Mr. Antiel boomed in his heartiest voice. "Don't tell me that we have a temperance advocate in our midst?" They all smiled at that, and even though Jenny knew that the remark didn't call for a reply she wished she had the courage to answer him honestly.

Her mother's glass was empty now. She handed it to Jenny. "Bring me another, will you, dear?"

Jenny stared at her in speechless astonishment and the blue eyes looked back at her soberly. Then her mother winked, such a faint wink that none of the others saw, no one but Jenny.

Moving woodenly, Jennifer went back to the kitchen. Her father was still fussing with the drinks, but he glanced at Jenny over his shoulder. "Mother's? There's a bottle of ginger ale in the refrigerator. Better put some more ice in it, too." He grinned at Patsy, who was following on Jennifer's heels. "How about you, Pat? Could you hold some more Coke or will it ruin your dinner?"

He brushed past with the glasses for Mr. and Mrs. Antiel and almost before the door swung behind him Jennifer lifted her mother's glass to sniff the contents and then taste it. She whirled around, her face glowing, to smile at Patsy. "Why . . . why, it's just plain ginger ale and ice," she said. "Mother's drinking ginger ale."

Patsy shrugged. "Maybe she didn't feel like having anything else. She doesn't have ulcers, does she?"

"Ulcers?"

"Yes, ulcers. My Uncle Jim has them and that's why he doesn't drink anything stronger than iced tea, he says."

Jennifer filled her mother's glass with ginger ale and ice cubes and then took it back to her, carrying the glass carefully and lovingly between her two hands, as if she were bearing a precious chalice.

She went out of her way to be especially charming to Mr. and Mrs. Antiel for the remainder of their visit. Patsy commented on it when the four grownups had driven off in the new convertible.

"What came over you, Jenny?" she asked accusingly. "I didn't think you liked those people at all, and then all of a sudden butter wouldn't melt in your mouth. What happened?"

Jennifer sighed. "I don't know," she said, not quite truthfully. "You don't suppose all that sweetness and light of yours is beginning to rub off on me, do you?"

"What sweetness and light?" Patsy gasped.

"Oh . . . you know . . . that business about not hurting people's feelings, and detouring around the truth if it's likely to be the least bit painful."

They prepared dinner and talked and giggled and exchanged confidences all through the long lazy evening.

"Do you ever feel that you've reached a place in your life when you wished that everything would just *stop?*" Jenny asked dreamily, as they sat side by side on the front step, watching the slow-moving traffic and calling friendly hello's to the people walking past. And then, as Patsy looked at her with puzzled eyes, she hastened to explain. "I mean, do you ever feel that everything is just about perfect and you'd like to keep it that way for years and years? One day exactly like another?"

Patsy shook her head. "I can't say I ever have. I don't think I'd like it, having one day exactly like the day before. It'd get awfully monotonous."

Jennifer pulled her knees up to her chin and tucked her skirt carefully around her. "Monotony has its points, though."

"Yes, but just think of staying the same age!" Patsy argued. "Being sixteen forever and ever. Just a little too young to be completely grown-up and too old to enjoy being a child. That would be pretty grim, don't you think?"

"I guess so," Jennifer said, smiling. "If you say so."

When they went into the living room an hour or so later, to look up some of Jennifer's father's old phonograph records, Patsy pounced upon the photograph album that was stored on the same shelf.

"Oh, hey! Family pictures! I love them.'

"The trouble with family pictures," Jennifer said, "is that they aren't interesting to anyone outside the family."

"Don't be silly. I'm not family and I love family pic—" She stopped suddenly, her blue eyes stricken. "Look, if you don't want me to look at them. . . ." She put down the album so hastily that Jennifer was ashamed of her own reluctance. "I'm sorry, Jenny." She looked so acutely uncomfortable that Jennifer hastened to reassure her.

"It's all right, Patsy." Jenny picked up the album and held it against her heart in a childish gesture. "I guess it's just that when you're right in the middle of a new life you sort of hate to start thinking about the old one."

"Then we won't start thinking about it," Patsy said quickly.

Jennifer opened the first page of the book, and the familiar photograph of two solemn-eyed babies looked out at the two girls. "This is me with my twin sister Molly," Jenny said. "She died a long time ago, when she was just eight years old."

Patsy looked startled. "Your sister? Your *twin* sister? Why, Jenny, I thought you were an only child."

"And so I am," Jenny replied gently. "Look, here are some more pictures of us. Weren't we cute?"

They sat down side by side on the davenport and Jennifer turned the pages one by one. "I don't remember where most of these were taken, but this one, when we were about five or six, was taken at Coney Island. I remember that one. I think I remember it. We went on a picnic, just Mother and Dad and Molly and me. It was the middle of the summer and awfully hot and crowded but we must have enjoyed it. Did you ever see such absolutely blissful expressions?"

They tipped their heads forward studying the picture and Patsy giggled. "You were just darling. Which one is you, Jenny? Or do you know?"

"Of course I know. I'm the one on the right." She squinted at the picture doubtfully. "Or maybe the left. Anyway I'm one of them." She turned another page. "And will you look at this? Ballet skirts! That was taken when we were in Miss Freeley's dancing school."

There was another picture of the two girls ready for school. Carrying brand-new lunch boxes and book bags, wearing identical jackets and beanies and self-conscious smiles.

"That was one of the last pictures we had of Molly.

It was just a little bit after that that she was killed." Jenny closed the book and looked up to meet her friend's sober eyes.

"You must have missed her terribly, Jenny."

"Yes. I still miss her. It's funny, but . . . since we've lived here I haven't missed her quite so much."

They went back into Jennifer's room and listened to some more records and it wasn't until they heard her parents drive in that Jenny remembered she hadn't put away the photograph album.

Her mother's eyes found the shabby book almost at once as she came into the living room, dropped her coat over the back of a chair, and turned to smile at the two girls in the hallway. "Oh, you've been showing Patsy our pictures," she said mildly. "Did she bore you to death, Pat?"

"Oh, no. I loved seeing them. I was the one who insisted."

Mrs. Martin tossed a quick smile in Jenny's direction. "Did you kids have a good time? Did you find enough to eat?"

"Oh, yes, we're stuffed," Patsy assured her.

Mrs. Martin put the photograph album away without even glancing inside. She went on talking in the same cheerful voice, and when the girls went to bed she came in and tucked them both in just as if they were both hers.

"Did you have a nice time, Mother?" Jenny asked, as her mother's soft kiss brushed her cheek.

"Yes, dear, a very nice time. Mr. Antiel and your father didn't have much time to talk business, but I could see that they liked each other."

"They liked you, too. Both Mr. and Mrs. Antiel."

"And they thought you were charming," Jennifer's mother said lightly. "So now with our mutual admiration society disposed of, shall we say good night?"

"Your mother's fun," Patsy observed over a contented yawn, when the door closed and the room was dark again. "Sometimes she acts about our age, but then other times. . . ." She stopped and then continued lamely, "Well, like tonight, for instance, when she was talking to those people, her eyes looked about a million years old."

"They did?" Jennifer spoke faintly. "I didn't notice."

"Oh, I guess when you're close to a person all the time you get sort of used to the way they look. Maybe it's because of Molly that she looks like that . . . sometimes."

"Like what?" Jennifer persisted.

"Sort of sad and hungry," Patsy said, and then gave a quick self-conscious giggle. "That sounds sort of odd, but she does have the exact same expression that my mother gets after she's been on one of her diets for about a week and has to prepare meals for the rest of us."

Jennifer was silent. She was silent for so long that Patsy at last decided that she had fallen asleep.

Chapter Six

A COUPLE of days later, Griff Nolan fell into step beside Jennifer as she was hurrying toward the lunchroom.

"Hi!" he said. "You look as if you're going somewhere important. Can I tag along?"

Her steps slowed and her eyes widened in surprise. "I'm just going down to have lunch."

"Same here." He held up his lunch sack to show her and then took her arm to help her wind her way through the maze of students coming from the opposite direction. "The traffic situation in these halls is getting worser and worser," he complained goodnaturedly. "Every month or so we get a new set of rules. March on the right side of the halls, keeping close to the walls, unless you are making a left-hand turn, in which case you will form a second line, parallel with the first. *Unless* you are going in both directions at once, in which case, of course, you will confer with the nearest monitor." He broke off and shrugged. "Well, anyway, it goes something like that."

Jennifer nodded. "At least it makes as much sense as this traffic snarl." She glanced back over her shoulder to see if Patsy was coming. They usually had lunch together, but this afternoon Patsy was walking beside Elsie McNeill, talking so earnestly that she didn't even notice Jennifer.

It was fun to find herself seated beside Griff at the long table in the middle of the lunchroom, fun to be part of the noisy gang she had been watching and secretly envying all these weeks. Elsie and Patsy found places farther along the table and Jenny waved at them. Her first uneasy feeling that Patsy was annoyed about something was dispelled when she tossed a rosy apple the length of the lunch table. "Here, Jenny, catch!"

"Thanks, Pat!" She captured the apple and put it on the pile with the rest of the loot that was accumulating before her. Her own lunch sack had been opened and passed around, the other boys and girls were sampling her tuna sandwiches and cookies, and Griff had calmly confiscated her bag of potato chips. "Doesn't anyone ever eat their own lunch around here?" she asked, not complaining, just being curious.

"Of course not! How dull," someone said, and

reached over and exchanged the apple for an orange.

Jennifer looked around and smiled and answered the questions that were shot at her. She felt comfortable and thoroughly at home with all these strangers, and she couldn't help wondering if maybe, just maybe, it wasn't because Griff seemed to have taken over the job of making her one of them. She watched Griff and laughed at his corny jokes and grinned her approval of the foolish antics that went on around the table.

"Ever play gossip, Jenny?" someone asked, and when she admitted that she hadn't they at once launched into the game.

"It's perfectly simple," Griff explained to Jenny in a hurried aside, as the gossip traveled the length of the table. "The first one on the left side of the table whispers something to the next one to him and then that one relays the message to the next one and so on and so on till we get to the end of the line."

The gossip traveled one side of the table and crossed to Jenny's side. When the girl next to her whispered in Jennifer's ear it sounded as if she said, "The girl was standing under the mistletoe." Jenny relayed this information faithfully to Griff, but by the time it had reached the end of the table it had become, "The girl was standing. I think she missed the boat!"

Everyone roared with laughter when it was discovered that the original gossip was "Muriel Standish has a lovely fur coat."

They were all having fun, Jennifer thought; they were all so friendly and uncomplicated. Everyone seemed to know Griff and look up to him.

"Here, Griff! You like bananas. Catch!"

"Hey, Griff! What about that math review? Do you think you passed?"

"Griff Nolan, can't you toss some weight around and get them to do something about those ancient records in the jukebox? Some of those numbers are so archaic my *folks* used to dance to them!"

Griff had time for everything and everybody. His brown eyes twinkled as he teased one of the girls about her pineapple haircut. "Holy smokes, Marge! I saw you coming out of the girls' gym and I thought one of the fellows had wandered out of bounds. How come you let them scalp you, honey?"

Marge made a little face at him. "Oh, you're just in a rut! Larry likes my hair this way, don't you, Larry?"

Larry nodded. "I do if you say so—I guess," he said cautiously.

They all laughed and someone made a joke about Larry's being henpecked. Larry and Marge were two of the crowd who were going steady. Jennifer had discovered that several young couples belonged to this select company.

It was easy to sort out the girls who were going steady. They wore boys' rings, not on their fingers but on heavy chains around their necks. The boys were a little harder to identify. You had to wait and see which boy gravitated to the side of a girl wearing a ring.

Privately Jennifer thought it was all a little silly. If you liked a boy and he liked you, that ought to be enough. You ought to be able to go out together and have fun, without having to wear the boy's ring like a no-trespassing sign. That was one of the questions that was always being hotly debated whenever a bunch of girls got together. So far Jennifer had managed to stay tactfully on the side lines.

When they had finished eating and were ready to return to their afternoon classes, Griff walked along with Jennifer as naturally as if they'd known one another for years and years.

Why he *likes* me, Jennifer thought happily. Maybe he likes the way I look or maybe he thinks I'm fun or maybe he's impressed by our convertible, the way Patsy was.

It would have been nice to be able to ask him if there was any special reason why he had singled her out. She smiled, a crooked little smile that nudged her lips and deepened the dimple in one cheek. Griff noticed it at once. "You're grinning about something," he said. "Tell me."

She shook her head. "Just girl stuff. A man wouldn't understand." She could see that he was pleased at being referred to as a man. Honestly, boys were *so* transparent.

"What about that party at Mike's this week end?" Griff asked as they paused at the top of the stairs before continuing on to their classes. "That Halloween affair."

"What about it?"

"I was wondering if you were planning to go."

Jenny looked surprised. "Why . . . why, no, Griff. I don't even know Mike."

"It's one of those deals where a fellow is supposed to invite a girl," Griff explained in an elaborately casual tone. "I was just thinking—if no one else had asked you—and you think you might like to go, I mean, would you like to go with me?"

"I'd love to go," Jennifer told him, her eyes shining. "But I'll have to find out if it's all right with my mother first."

"Of course," Griff said. "I'll get Mike's mother to call yours if you think that might help. I know all about mothers."

They exchanged quick grins. "It sounds dreamy,"

Jennifer said, and glanced covertly at her watch. "Oh, I have to dash now, Griff, or I'll be late for class."

"O.K. I'll call you tonight, hmm?"

"Yes. Do that, and keep your fingers crossed that Mother's in a good mood." They hurried off in opposite directions and Jennifer caught up with Patsy, who had brushed past her without stopping. "Hey, where's the fire? You snubbing me or something?"

Patsy's blue eyes met hers directly. "Of course I'm not snubbing you. I just didn't want to barge in."

"Barge in, for pity's sake!" Jenny grinned at her friend engagingly. "Griff was just inviting me to a Halloween party. At Mike Somebody-or-other's. Will you be going, Patsy?"

Patsy knitted her eyebrows comically. "Mike Somebody-or-other. No, I don't believe I know him. He must be a cousin of Wha'dya-call-him or What's-his-name."

The bell ended the ridiculous conversation and Jennifer went to her desk still grinning. For some reason they never did resume the subject of Griff's inviting Jennifer to the party.

That afternoon Patsy stayed for basketball practice and Jenny found herself walking home with Elsie McNeill. Elsie was also going to the party at Mike's house. It turned out that Mike had a last name—Johnson. Jennifer filed this bit of information to relay to her mother. Griff had said that Mike's mother would call and talk to hers.

"I think this is the nicest, *friendliest* town," Jennifer confided as a car roared by filled with yelling teen-agers, all of whom called greetings to both girls. "In a big city you never get to really *know* the kids you go to school with, not like this, with mothers calling up other mothers just to check a party."

"Oh, Mrs. Johnson is terribly Emily Post about things like that," Elsie said. "She screens Mike's friends pretty thoroughly, to be sure that no unhealthy element creeps in."

"Unhealthy element?"

"Oh, you know, juvenile delinquents. Or those who come from bad stock." Elsie shrugged and grimaced. "Search me, I'm only quoting Mrs. Johnson. She's really a drip, Jenny, I may as well warn you, but she does give good parties. The food is fabulous and they have a yummy recreation room for dancing and play-ing records and just sitting around yakking." Elsie shifted her books from one arm to the other and heaved an exaggerated sigh. "I just hope she doesn't have a bunch of dopey games lined up for us to play. Do you like to dance, Jenny?"

"I've never gone to a *real* dance," Jenny confessed apologetically. "I mean a dress-up dance with a boy and a corsage and everything."

Elsie stared at her. "Well, who *has?* The dances we go to are just this kind of thing. Sometimes we have school mixers, but not too often. Usually the boys line up on one side of the gym and the girls line up on the other side and they just sort of stare at each other all evening."

"It sounds fascinating," Jenny said.

"Oh, it is," Elsie agreed. "And the minute the clock strikes ten the chaperons heave a sigh of relief and send us all home."

They walked along for another block and then Elsie came back to the subject. "A couple of years ago there was a Junior Ballroom deal in town. A couple of dancing teachers came in and gave lessons and sponsored a dance once a week. It folded up after a couple of weeks, though; not enough boys joined the class, and there were the girls all waltzing around and around together."

"It sounds pretty dull," Jenny said sympathetically.

"Of course as soon as we're seventeen we can go to the Beach Club dances. If our parents happen to belong, that is. Mine don't."

Jennifer had the feeling that it wouldn't be very tactful to mention that her father *did* belong to the Beach Club. She changed the subject by leaning forward and examining the ring that Elsie was wearing on a chain about her neck.

"Isn't this a going-steady ring?" she asked curiously.

"Yes. Bill gave it to me the week after school started." Elsie sounded a little smug. "Honestly, Jennifer, you have no idea what a relief it is. Not having to worry about whether someone will invite you to things like this party of Mike's." She fingered the ring complacently as she went on. "Mother had an absolute fit the first time she noticed that I was wearing it, but I finally managed to convince her that it was the only solution. And after all, going steady isn't the same as being engaged."

"It isn't?" Jenny sounded a little dubious. "Then what's the point of going steady?"

Elsie shrugged. "Well . . . going steady is . . . just going steady, I guess. Not going out with other fellows and always having one boy available to take you to parties or to the movies, or even just come and sit around and watch television with you." She sounded a little vague.

Jennifer still wasn't satisfied with her answer. "Do you mean that being engaged is planning to be married and going steady is planning to be engaged? Is that it?"

"I guess so." Elsie still sounded doubtful. "Do you have to analyze it? I just know that in a little town like this you have to have someone you can depend on. You're liable to be left high and dry if you don't have a steady. And if you start playing the field, the way a new girl does sometimes, you just get the reputation of being a flirt."

"Do you now?" The laughter deepened in Jenny's voice. She knew that she had received fair warning. Not that Elsie needed to worry. No one had to worry about Jennifer Martin. She wanted nothing better than to conform to whatever established patterns were pointed out to her. "I hate to be a wet blanket," she went on after a moment, "but this going-steady racket seems pretty contrived to me. Take you, for example. You don't even sound as if you like Bill very much."

"Oh, Bill's all right, I guess," Elsie said casually. "He's better than no one."

"I'd call that a pretty mild compliment," Jennifer observed. "Tell me, does Bill share this mad passion of yours?"

Elsie shrugged her shoulders and raised her eyebrows simultaneously. "Search me. All I know is that he's usually around."

Jennifer told her mother all about it as soon as she got home. Perched on the kitchen stool, watching her roll out pie crust and fit it neatly into a shell, she told her about Griff's having lunch with her and asking her to the party, about Elsie and Bill, who were going steady, even though Elsie didn't really like Bill very much. About Mike, whose last name was Johnson.

"I'll have to call Pat and ask her all about it—the party, I mean. She knows everyone. And Mike's mother is going to call you, Mother, did I mention that? So that you'll know that the party is going to be well chaperoned and everything."

"That's nice," Jennifer's mother said.

"Well, aren't you even excited?" Jenny demanded plaintively. "Do you realize that here I am past sixteen years old and this is the first time I ever had a date with a boy?"

Mrs. Martin looked at the glowing face and smiled. "Yes, honey, I realize it. I hope you go to your party and have a marvelous time, but don't let yourself be snowballed into going with just one boy even if it is the fashion. Look around a little and find out if this—what was his name? Oh, yes, Griff. Find out if he really is the one you're going to like to have around."

"But Griff hasn't asked me to go steady or anything like that," Jennifer protested in a scandalized voice. "Don't jump to conclusions like that! We're not eloping, you know. We're just going to this one party."

"That's what you said," her mother agreed mildly. "I just tossed in the advice for free."

"Because . . . well honestly . . . I don't even know why Griff asked me. Just about any of the girls would be glad to go with him, but he asked *me*."

Her mother smiled at her again. "You do have a mirror in your room, don't you, honey?"

Jennifer grinned and threw out both hands in a laughing self-deprecating gesture. "O.K. So I'm a living doll! Would it occur to you that you might be a little prejudiced?"

"I suppose so." Mrs. Martin returned her attention to the pie on the drainboard and started fluting the crust rapidly. "Well, it just so happens that you aren't the only member of the family who had a social success today. Margaret Ferris had a Milk Fund luncheon at her house this afternoon, and the ladies have invited me to join their circle."

"Are you going to?" Jennifer asked cautiously. "I thought . . . well, you said you thought those hen-party affairs were pretty ghastly." Too late she remembered that it had been a long time since her mother had said anything like that. Months and months. Before they even moved here.

"I seem to have changed my mind," her mother admitted calmly. "When you live in a community you have to be part of it. And the Milk Fund Circles do an excellent job. I was really surprised to hear the reports at today's meeting."

"What do they do?" Jenny asked, because she could see that her mother was dying to talk about it. "Roll bandages? Drink tea? Play bridge?"

"They sponsor some wonderful projects, mostly for orphan children. At Christmas time each of the women who has the room will take one of the children for Christmas week. Give them a real family Christmas. Doesn't it sound like a marvelous idea?"

"It certainly does! I hope you spoke up for one, Mother. Think how much fun it would be to have a little boy or girl around the house."

Her mother's eyes swung to Jennifer's face wistfully. "Do you really think so, Jenny?"

"I think it's a marvelous idea," Jenny repeated firmly. "Try to get a little girl about three or four. They're so cunning at that age!"

"It isn't quite that simple, darling. You just apply for a child and take the one you get. Mrs. Jenkins— that's the president of the Circle—was telling me this afternoon that they had the same project last year and three of the children were adopted into the families they visited."

"Well, we don't have to plan *that* far ahead," Jennifer reminded her mother. "Right now the big problem on the agenda is what I should wear to this affair Saturday night. I didn't even think to ask Elsie whether it's a sweater-and-skirt affair or more dress up. I know—I'll call Patsy about it. Patsy knows everything."

She got down off the stool and went into her room

and changed from her school clothes to the shirt and jeans she wore around the house. After she had finished her homework she called to see if Patsy was home from basketball practice yet.

Patsy herself answered the phone, but she wasn't her usual talkative self. She didn't seem at all thrilled about Jennifer's date, she didn't seem very much interested in Mike's party. It *could* be a case of sour grapes, of course, Jennifer told herself a little crossly after Patsy had explained that her mother was calling her and she had to hang up.

But somehow jealousy didn't fit into the picture that Jennifer had formed of her friend. Not Patsy, who had been so unaccountably delighted when Jennifer's drawings won praise from the difficult social-studies teacher. Not Patsy, who introduced her so proudly as "my friend, Jennifer Martin." Not Patsy, who had sponsored Jenny as a member of the exclusive Drama Club.

"She'll call back and explain why she was so abrupt," Jenny consoled herself as she went out into the kitchen to see if she could help. "She'll call after dinner."

But the evening passed without her doing so.

Griff called and talked for a while. Jennifer told him that Mrs. Johnson had already called her mother and that it was perfectly all right about the party.

"That's cool," Griff said. "I'll see you at school to-morrow. Gotta dash and do my homework now."

Jennifer didn't go to bed until almost ten, but Patsy still had not called.

Chapter Seven

IT was Elsie who cleared up the situation when they were walking to school the next day.

"Did your mother say that you could go to the party?" she asked at once, and when Jennifer said yes, that it was all settled, she grinned impishly. "What did Patsy say when you told her about it? Was she simply livid?"

"Why should she be livid?" Jenny demanded. "Because I'm going to a party?"

"Because you're going to a party with Griff Nolan," Elsie corrected her gleefully. "I'd just love to have seen her face when you told her."

Jennifer felt her heart plunge but she spoke casually. "She didn't say anything much, except that Griff was a lot of fun and that I'd probably have a marvelous time." She didn't know what had prompted her to tell the fib, but she was glad to see that Elsie looked vaguely disappointed.

After that they just talked about what they would wear to the party, and what kind of chance Central would have against their rival Fairview High, in the Thanksgiving Day game.

At the school entrance Elsie ran off to join some of the other girls, and Jennifer went to her locker to put away her jacket and the books she wouldn't be needing until the afternoon classes. A girl was struggling with the combination lock on her locker just a few steps away. It was a girl Jenny couldn't remember ever having seen before, so she was probably a transfer. Jennifer walked over to her and she looked up in some surprise, brushing the blond hair away from her cheek as she straightened, and making a little face at the jammed locker. "Darn thing just doesn't want to work. I even tried kicking it, but it still won't open."

"Do you have the combination written down?" Jennifer asked mildly. "Brute strength doesn't seem to impress these things." They both worked with the combination then, and after a while it opened. "There!" Jenny smiled at the new girl. "I'm Jennifer Martin. You're new, aren't you?"

"Yes. My brother and I are just starting today. We're from California. I'm Diane Winters . . . and I thank you very much."

"Glad I could help," Jennifer said. "I'm a Johnnycome-lately myself. I moved here from New York less than two months ago."

Jennifer went back to her own locker, took a swift appraising look at her face in the wavery mirror, and suppressed a deep sigh. Life was really pretty complicated. Why couldn't it have been some other boy who had invited her to Mike's party? She ought to have guessed what was the matter with Patsy. Why, Patsy had been the one who had introduced Griff to her in the first place; there had even been a faintly proprietary air about the introduction, now that she stopped to think about it.

Jennifer stacked the books on her arm with the depressed feeling that things were somehow spoiled. Patsy was her friend, her very good friend. She had gone out of her way to make Jennifer welcome, to include her in everything. And how was Jenny repaying her kindness? By waltzing off with Patsy's boy friend at the first opportunity.

Of course it wasn't quite like that. She hadn't sought out Griff; he was the one who had made all the friendly gestures. And it wasn't as if she'd known that Patsy liked Griff, if she did like him. She closed her locker finally and started down the hall.

Patsy came flying toward her from the other end of the long hallway. Her blue eyes were dancing and her brown curls stood on end.

"I ran all the way," she greeted Jennifer breathlessly. "That darn alarm clock again! And if I'm tardy just once more this semester I'm going to be put on clean-up detail in the lunchroom." She was hurling things into her locker as she spoke. "Here, be an angel, Jenny, and hold my books. You don't happen to have an extra pen, do you? I just remembered that mine is on the telephone stand at home."

Jenny got a pen from her purse and tucked it carefully into one of Patsy's books. "You can use this one, but don't forget where it came from. O.K.?"

"O.K.," Patsy agreed happily. "Come on! We'll have to zoom if we want to beat the bell."

Jennifer hurried along beside her, relieved that all the constraint was gone, that she and Patsy were friends again.

Maybe I just imagined that she acted funny yesterday, Jenny told herself, as she sped along at Patsy's heels. Maybe Elsie was just making all that up about Patsy's liking Griff.

The more she thought about it, i   vinced herself that she had been wo   Why, she and Patsy had been togethe   constantly these past weeks and Patsy had never once hinted that there was a special boy she was interested in. A girl would just naturally talk about something like that unless . . . unless . . . well, suppose she had liked Griff, but he hadn't liked her. She wouldn't do much talking about that.

Jennifer discussed the problem with her mother that evening. Patsy had come in to do homework with her, and it was after she had gathered up her books and started home that Jenny spoke to her mother. "Mom, did Patsy seem a little strange to you this afternoon? As if . . . as if she might be hurt or upset about something?"

Her mother looked startled. "Why, no, dear, not that I noticed. Why? Should she feel hurt and upset about something?"

"I don't know," Jennifer admitted unhappily. She told her mother about the conversation with Elsie and how Patsy had seemed so odd about the party, not even wanting to talk about it.

Her mother was sympathetic but not very helpful. She thought that Jenny should come right out and ask   it.

"   an't do that! How would it sound? 'If   ur personal property I'll keep hands o'   with an ounce of pride would want him a   ."

"Maybe she doesn't want him anyway," Jennifer's mother pointed out sensibly. "But you could always go to the other extreme and simply tell Griff that you don't want to go to the party."

"But I *do* want to go," Jenny almost wailed. "I'm simply dying to go. If I don't go everyone will think I'm stuck-up and I'll never be asked again. I'll just sit around being a wallflower and an old maid for the rest of my life."

"Oh, I wouldn't count on that," her mother said placidly. "There must be a few other boys, as stupid as Griff, who'll invite you to go out with them from time to time."

Jennifer looked at her darkly, even though it was hard not to laugh. "That's what I like about mothers," she announced to the room at large. "They're so comforting!"

Griff came over on Friday evening, supposedly to help Jenny with some geometry problems but actually to meet her parents. He hadn't said he was coming and Jennifer was a little flustered when she answered the doorbell and found him standing there. He looked strange and adult, because he wasn't wearing the same jacket and slacks he wore at school, but a sport coat and blue serge trousers. He was even wearing a tie! His hair was combed within an inch of its life and his shoes were polished. He wore an air of gravity like a cloak that he might toss aside at any moment.

Jennifer invited him in and made the introductions, and then explained that Griff had dropped in to help her with some geometry problems. Even to herself it sounded ridiculous. Why should he dress in his Sunday best in order to sit in the kitchen with her and struggle with geometry?

But her parents accepted this explanation gravely, and after Griff and Jennifer were settled on each side of the kitchen table, their books strewn about with careless abandon, Mrs. Martin came in and dished up some ice cream for them and put the cooky jar within convenient reach.

Griff really didn't understand geometry any better than Jennifer did, but she was careful not to point this out. They did their assignments, arguing good-naturedly over the problems and once even calling Elsie to verify a formula that bothered both of them.

When the fights came on TV, Jennifer's father came and asked Griff if he wouldn't like to watch them.

"Thanks, sir, but I ought to be getting home as soon as we're finished with this last problem. Tomorrow night's the big party and my folks don't like the idea of my being out too many nights in a row."

He was so polite and so obviously on his best behavior that Jenny had to grin. Griff caught the tag end of the grin as he turned back to his work, and the moment the door had closed behind her father he looked at Jenny sternly. "Look," he said, "if you want me to, I can chew gum or smoke cigarettes or put my feet up on the furniture. Or I can talk out of the side of my mouth and call your father Pop."

"Why should I want you to do anything like that?" she demanded, startled.

"I wouldn't know. But so long as I *am* trying to make a good impression. . . ."

"And you are succeeding beyond your wildest dreams," Jennifer interrupted sweetly. "Why, I'm even impressed myself."

"See that you stay that way," he advised her. "As an expert on parents I take my hat off to no one." He smoothed back his hair so complacently that Jennifer promptly went into a fit of giggles.

"How come you're such an expert on parents?" she asked, when they were piling up their books, the lessons completed.

"Research," Griff told her solemnly. "I've studied thousands of case histories in my time."

They went into the front room and Griff said good-by to her parents while Jennifer got his sport coat from the hall closet. She walked out to the gate with him and they said good night there. There always seemed to be so many things to talk about when it was time to say good night.

"I may be a photographer on the *Shingle* staff. Did I tell you about that, Jenny?"

"No, you didn't tell me. But how exciting!"

Griff opened the gate. "About this doings tomorrow night," he said. "O.K. if I pick you up a little after eight?"

"That will be fine." Jennifer said. A dog barked sharply somewhere down the street and that reminded her of something else. "Oh, Griff, did I tell you that I've almost got Dad talked into buying me a puppy? We have such a perfect place for one here and I've never had a real live pet, except a canary once."

Griff grinned down at her. He was quite a bit taller, so that he had to duck his head forward. "That seems funny. We've always had a couple of dogs and usually a half dozen cats around the place. Not to mention turtles and hamsters and an aquarium of tropical fish. Mother can never bear to turn anything away from the house. That's how I got my first turtle. I slipped him in behind the screen door and then ran around and came in the house the other way, so that Mother'd be the one to find him."

Griff talked about his family like that once in a while, mentioning his mother or his father or his sister Marion. There was a younger brother, too, named Herbie. And a married sister whose name was Clare.

It was fun, filling in all the facts one at a time, fitting together all the assorted odds and ends of information. All the things that made Griff *Griff*, and different from anyone else. It even pleased her to think that Griff was fitting all the things about her into a pattern, too. A pattern that would explain why she was Jennifer.

She gestured toward the tree. "Did I ever introduce you to our tree, Griff? She's a member of the family."

Griff glanced over his shoulder and then back at her in some perplexity. "Did you ever introduce me to who?"

"Our tree. We're very fond of her."

Jennifer felt an almost painful need to make him understand how she felt about the tree.

"When we first moved here," she told him earnestly, "I thought it was the most marvelous thing in the world that we should own a tree. In fact, this tree is practically the main reason why Father bought the house."

After Griff had sauntered off, Jennifer stayed at the gate, leaning on it a little just to make it creak, thinking back over the evening and delaying the moment when she would go in and ask her mother and father how they had liked Griff. Before she went back into the house she went over to the tree and put her hand against it lightly. She looked up into the shadows and smiled and put her ear against the trunk to hear if there might be a sound like a heartbeat. Someone at school had told her that when the sap ran in the tree it sounded like that. She still didn't know whether they were teasing her, but anyway it was a nice notion.

Her mother opened the door and looked out. "Jenny? Someone on the phone, dear. I think it's Patsy."

It *was* Patsy and her voice sounded queer, far-off and husky. "I suppose you're all set for the party tomorrow night," she grumbled. "Wouldn't you just know I'd come down with this miserable cold?"

"But you were perfectly all right at school today," Jenny said, before she thought. "What happened?"

There was a little silence and then Patsy was explaining fluently, too fluently. "It's my own stupid fault. I was sitting right square in a draft during fifth period today, but I hated to complain so I just skipped it. I've been sneezing and sneezing." She sneezed again to prove her point, but it wasn't a very convincing sneeze. "I've been taking aspirin and stuff, but you know how these head colds are. Once you have them they just have to run their course."

"I suppose so."

"So . . . it looks as if the party will just have to struggle along without me," Patsy concluded dramatically.

"What about your date?" Jennifer asked, realizing at the same moment that Patsy hadn't actually said that she had one. "Will he be able to find another girl at the last minute?"

Patsy's laugh was hollow. "Jenny dear, they can *always* find another girl at the last minute. That's one of the sad things about boys."

Jennifer hung up the receiver thoughtfully. Patsy wasn't a very good liar. Probably no one had invited her to Mike's party. It was a sobering thought, because a girl as well liked and such fun to be with as Patsy shouldn't have any trouble getting dates. Maybe Elsie did have a point there about going steady.

She went back into the living room, where her parents were watching television. Her mother looked up with a quick smile. "Griff seems to be a nice boy. Did you finish all your geometry?"

"Yes. We polished it off nicely. The homework was just an excuse, though," Jennifer admitted. "He really came so that you and Dad could look him over."

"That was thoughtful of him," Jennifer's mother said. "He has lovely manners."

Jennifer looked at her father, who had offered no comment. "Did you like him, Father?" she asked pointedly.

For just a moment her father looked uncomfortable and then he gave a little shrug. "Personally," he said, "I don't care to be addressed as 'sir.' Makes me feel as though I should be sporting a long gray beard."

Jennifer grinned. "Well, of course those were his company manners. They were meant to impress you."

"They did," he said, and the way he said it made it clear that it was not a compliment.

Jennifer couldn't help being pleased that her father had refused to fit into Griff's preconceived ideas of how a parent should react. Not that she wanted her father to dislike Griff, of course, but she still felt a little smug because he hadn't been charmed by Griff, the self-styled expert on parents.

Chapter Eight

Jᴇɴɴɪꜰᴇʀ was ready a little before eight, but she stayed in her room until eight-thirty, peeking out through the curtains once in a while, expecting momentarily to see Griff come swinging along the street and turning in at the gate.

Her mother came in after a while and sat down on the edge of the bed to talk to her. She told Jenny, once again, how nice she looked. "I'm so glad this turned out to be a dress-up party," she confided. "I guess I just belong to the old-fashioned school that believes girls should look feminine and pretty whenever possible."

Jenny nodded thoughtfully and whirled about before the full-length mirror. Her skirt fanned out over the billow of petticoats. "It's funny you should say that, because I was just wondering what I'm going to do with a dozen stick-out petticoats if full skirts go out of fashion."

"Don't worry about it, honey. We can always sew them together and use them for curtains," her mother said.

They were both just making conversation to cover the uneasy fact that Griff was late. Jenny wondered what she would do if he didn't show up.

"Oh, heavenly day, my nail polish!" She said it as if it were something terribly important, like forgetting her shoes. "I'll put it on now and Griff will just have to wait, that's all."

It sounded as if she really hadn't expected Griff to be prompt, and she took her time about getting out the bottle of polish and settling herself carefully on the dressing-table bench. She applied the pale-pink lacquer slowly and painstakingly, but with every stroke of the brush she was straining her ears for the sound of hurried footsteps along the walk or quick feet crossing the porch, for the sound of the doorbell and then Griff's voice asking her father if Jennifer was ready.

The phone rang once, and both Jennifer and her mother listened as her father answered. Jennifer started to breathe again when she realized that the call was for him, something about business. Still, it wouldn't have hurt Griff to at least telephone if he was going to be delayed. He might be trying to reach her now, this minute, while her father was talking to

some man who could just as well call him at the office.
But after a moment her father concluded his conversation and returned to his TV program, and still Griff
didn't call.

It was almost nine before he got there, and instead
of the apologies and explanations she halfway expected, Griff merely reminded her that the party had
started at eight and they'd better hurry.

"*I've* been ready for fifteen minutes," she told him
a little stiffly.

"Well, good for you! I like gals to be punctual."
His grin was teasing her. Then he said, "Jenny, you
look like a million dollars!" and she forgave him immediately.

They walked to the party; it was just a few blocks
away.

"Sometimes I can borrow Dad's car, if he's in a good
mood or I've been on my good behavior. But I hate
to crowd my luck and I didn't think you'd mind walking tonight. It's such a swell night." He looked down
at her questioningly and Jenny nodded.

"Oh, yes, I love to walk. Back home Mother and I
used to take long walks almost every night. That was
when Dad was out here getting settled and time was
hanging heavy on our hands." She gave a little skip
to keep up with him and Griff slowed down. "We used
to just crawl along because it was so hot and sticky,

but walking was better than just sitting, and after all you can't spend all your time in air-conditioned movies."

Griff squinted at her. "You and your mother are pretty close, aren't you? I mean, I never hear you complaining about how she interferes in your life, the way the other girls do."

"Yes, we are pretty close, I guess," Jenny conceded. "I imagine it's because I'm the only one."

"That doesn't follow," Griff informed her. "Look at Elsie. She's an only child, too, and she and her mother fight like strange bulldogs."

"Do they?"

"Oh, boy, do they! You can hear them clear down to Post Street. But you always act as if your mother was your sister or something, maybe a younger sister. The way you're always building her up, the way you always seem to be looking out for her."

"Oh, I don't either," Jenny protested quickly, and then added lamely, "Do I?"

Griff laughed. "Well, that business about being so excited because your mother was asked to join that Milk Fund deal! As if it was something special. And the way you led her around at the PTA meeting, introducing her to people and making sure that she wasn't left alone a minute."

"Anything else?" Jennifer asked calmly.

"Yep," Griff said cheerfully. "I think you probably have a mother complex. You even brag about her cooking, as if there was something spectacular about a woman knowing how to bake pies or cookies or cakes."

"I didn't realize I was being such a bore," Jennifer said stiffly.

Griff reached for her hand and swung it with his. "Hey, you don't have to apologize. I think it's cute. It isn't every day you meet a girl with a mother fixation."

She was mollified but still a little uneasy. She would have to watch it. If people were noticing this protectiveness, it was bound to make them wonder. She slanted a quick smile up at Griff. "Mother was ill for quite a while. I guess I'm just so relieved to have her herself again. . . ." She let the words trail off, but she could see that he had accepted the explanation.

The party was in full swing when they arrived, and they were at once absorbed into the party atmosphere. Mike's mother was a roly-poly little woman who greeted Jennifer warmly. "So you're the new girl we've been hearing about. From way back East Mike tells me. How do you like the wild and woolly West by now, my dear?"

Jennifer smiled. "Well, I have to confess that it isn't

as wild and woolly as I'd expected, after television," she said.

"The girls are leaving their coats in the room at the head of the stairs," Mrs. Johnson told her. "A couple of them are up there now, fixing their faces, I imagine. Why don't you run up and put your coat on the bed and then come down and join the party? I must see about the food situation." She bustled off and Jennifer, after a glance over her shoulder to see what had happened to Griff, went up the wide carpeted stairway.

The girls in the front bedroom were vaguely familiar to Jennifer. They introduced themselves and Jennifer told them who she was.

"Oh, yes. Jennifer Martin. The new girl from back East," one of them said. "You came with Griff Nolan, didn't you?"

Jennifer said yes, that she was Griff's date.

"It figures," the other girl said under her breath, and then had the grace to blush when Jennifer looked at her curiously.

"Might as well get back to the party," the first girl broke in hurriedly. "You coming, Jennifer?"

Jennifer trailed after them down the stairs and then down another flight of stairs that ended in the big recreation room. She saw Elsie across the room and waved at her, but Elsie was arguing with Bill about something and scarcely took the time to smile in return. Griff was already in a corner with some of the other boys, talking football. He grinned at Jennifer, but made no move to come across the room and see that she met everyone. It was all right, though; she knew most of the boys and girls, and even the names that weren't familiar belonged to faces that she had passed dozens of times in the corridors at school.

As Elsie had feared, their hostess was equipped with games to play. Mostly paper games that called forth a good deal of discussing back and forth and eliminated any possible feeling of competition. "Hey, look! Sam's got number ten. Sam, I'll trade you that answer for number four." "I know that one but I can't spell it. Does *manufacture* have any double letters, does anyone know?"

Mrs. Johnson was visibly disturbed by all this casual conversation. "Everyone is supposed to get his own answer," she kept saying. "That's cheating, Mike. Don't you dare look at Sally's paper."

Jennifer applied herself to the word game and finally turned in her paper before half the others had finished clowning around. Mrs. Johnson scarcely glanced at the answers before announcing loudly that Jennifer had won, and now they would have the scavenger hunt.

There was a chorus of groans. "Mrs. Johnson, do we

have to?" one of the brave ones asked. "It's so cold out and my mother will just have a fit if I start my asthma again."

Mrs. Johnson looked upset. "Why, David, I never heard that you were bothered with asthma. Be sure to have your mother call me tomorrow, and I'll tell her about this perfectly wonderful steam treatment my doctor recommends."

Someone had turned on the record player and a couple started to dance. Other couples joined them and a barber shop quartet in the corner added their voices to the din. Some of the girls went upstairs to comb their hair, and the football discussion was resumed. Every few minutes Mrs. Johnson asked plaintively if they wouldn't like to go on the scavenger hunt now, but Jennifer had the feeling she really didn't care much whether they went or not.

Jennifer sat on the floor with a couple of the other girls and helped sort records. Most of the records had little strips of adhesive on them bearing a name. Jennifer learned that all the boys and girls had brought their favorite records from home.

"Oh, someone should have told me," she said. "I have a lot of good ones. Maybe—maybe next time. . . ."

"Hear that, gang? Jennifer has slugs of new records. Let's make her go home and get them."

They were just joking, though, they told her, when

Jennifer was willing to oblige. They'd catch her for the next party. For the next party. As if she were already one of them.

"Where's Pat?" someone asked a little later in the evening, and it seemed to Jennifer that there was an uneasy little silence after she had explained that Patsy had a bad cold.

"That reminds me," one of the boys remarked slyly. "Have you seen the new chick? She's a junior." Then he turned on Griff. "Come on now, Griff. *You* must have noticed her?"

For a startled moment Jennifer saw that Griff was really angry. Then he managed a smile and turned to include her. "Can't say I've seen the gal. I must have been thinking about something else."

When the music started again he came over and pulled Jennifer to her feet and they danced. He wasn't an especially good dancer but Jennifer didn't mind.

The going-steady couples danced more than the other couples, she noted, and wondered if this might not be some faint argument in favor of the relationship. Maybe when you were going steady you could insist that the boy learn to dance even when his taste ran more to rehashing baseball averages and discussing all-American football candidates.

She tried to think what it would be like to be going steady with Griff. Bossing him around the way Elsie was bossing the hapless Bill, or dancing dreamily cheek to cheek like Marge and Larry. Then the thought of Patsy intruded and she felt a little disloyal.

She thanked Mrs. Johnson warmly when it was time for the party to break up. She even thanked Mike, who looked surprised and somewhat embarrassed. At the very last moment Mrs. Johnson remembered that Jennifer hadn't been given her prize for winning the word game and hurried upstairs to get it. They all watched as Jennifer unwrapped the package.

"It jingles," she announced, holding the package to her ear and shaking it. "Let's guess what it is."

"A pair of nylons," someone said immediately. "A mink stole." "A piano." "A tuna fish sandwich." "Oh, Jenny, for goodness sakes, open it."

It turned out to be a small copper bell. A dinner bell, Mrs. Johnson told her. "You can put it in your hope chest, honey. Or don't girls have hope chests any more?"

"It's lovely," Jennifer assured her sincerely. "Thank you so much, Mrs. Johnson." She tucked the package into her coat pocket, but several times on the way home she put her hand in her pocket and shook the box, delighting in the faint silvery tinkle of the bell.

Griff walked her home. There were four couples who started off together, but one by one they went in different directions and at last Griff and Jennifer were walking alone together through the dark, moonless night.

Griff reached over and took her hand and swung it lightly with his own. Once he looked down and grinned at her in the mushrooming light of a street lamp. "Your hand is sure little," he said. "Like holding a puppy's paw, sort of limp and boneless."

She wrinkled her nose. "I'm not sure I like that. I'll have to think about it for a while and let you know."

"You do that," he said cheerfully.

When they reached her house Jennifer hesitated for a moment before pushing the gate open.

"Do I leave you here?" he asked, reading her mind with painful accuracy. "Or am I supposed to walk up to the porch with you?"

Her shoulders lifted in a little shrug. "Search me. This is the first time we ever had a gate."

They both started to laugh, just as if this had been a terribly witty remark, and then they went up the walk and across the porch hand in hand. She started to reach for the doorknob, knowing that the door wouldn't be locked, but Griff's hand on her arm stopped the gesture.

"Hey, what's the big rush?" He turned her around then, and holding her firmly by the shoulders he kissed her—a swift, light kiss. "There!" he said. "That was for good night. Are you mad?"

She shook her head, smiling faintly, and he kissed her again. Not so swiftly this time; not so lightly, either.

"There!" he said again. "*That* was for not being mad."

She stood on the porch watching him until he had pushed through the gate and turned down the sidewalk. Even his footsteps, melting away into the night noises, were gay and self-assured, like Griff himself.

Her father was reading when she peeked into the living room, but he laid aside his magazine so quickly that she knew he hadn't been much interested in it, that it was just an excuse to stay up until she was in.

"Well, hi, honey! How was the party?" he asked.

"We had a ball," Jennifer assured him. "Real crazy. Where's Mother?"

"She just went out to make some hot chocolate. Do you want to ask her to make it three?"

Jennifer made a face. "Ugh! No! We simply ate and ate at the party. I feel as if I won't want to eat again for a week."

Her father was watching her narrowly. "But you did have a good time?"

"Oh, yes. I really did. Everyone was so nice. And

they said next time I must bring my records, so I guess they'll invite me again."

"Of course they'll invite you again," he said, in a tone that indicated he'd never doubted it for an instant. "But maybe you can turn the tables and invite all of them to a party here. We have plenty of room, and you could fill the refrigerator with Cokes and take up the rugs for dancing. Maybe the Christmas holidays would be a good time. What do you think?"

She avoided his eyes carefully as she spoke. "Well, maybe later on when they know me a little better. I don't want them to think I'm rushing things."

Her mother came in, carrying the two steaming cups carefully. "Oh, good!" she said. "You're home. Can we sell you some hot chocolate?"

Jennifer shook her head and repeated what she had told her father. "We simply ate and ate all evening long. I don't want to even think about food for a week."

"Was it fun? Did you have a good time?" her mother asked, after she had given her husband his cup and crossed to her own chair.

"Oh, yes, it was a wonderful party. And look—I even won a prize." She took the package from her coat pocket and proudly displayed the copper bell. "Isn't it pretty? Mrs. Johnson said I could put it in my hope chest." She tinkled the bell and then put it back in the box. "We were supposed to go on a scavenger hunt, too, but most of the kids didn't want to. They said they were tired of scavenger hunts."

"What a shame! I used to think they were fun. Well, what else did you do that was fun, besides not going on the scavenger hunt?"

"Oh, we danced . . . some of the couples danced . . . and we all sat around and talked a lot and we listened to records and . . . well, just things like that." She yawned and stretched, slipping her arms out of her coat. "Guess I'll go to bed. Morning comes early." She kissed them both and went to her room.

She got ready for bed unhurriedly, thinking back over the evening and reliving some of the best moments. Frowning a little, she remembered the way the girl had said, "It figures," when she learned that Jennifer was Griff's date. Maybe she had a crush on Griff, maybe she was just jealous. But Jennifer's innate honesty kept her from really believing that. And there had been the bit when the boy teased Griff about the new blonde at school. And the awkward moment after Patsy's name was mentioned.

When she was in bed her mother came in to kiss her good night again and checked to be sure the window was open. "I'm glad you had a good time, honey," she murmured against Jennifer's cheek. "We . . . your father and I want you to like living here."

"Oh, I do like it," Jennifer said drowsily. "I love it. Everyone is so friendly, and just think, I'm going to know these same kids all my life. We'll graduate together and some of us will get married and have children and go right on living in this same little town forever and ever."

Her mother smiled in the darkness. Jennifer could hear the smile in her voice. "Take it easy, Jenny," she said. "We can wait a few more years before we start planning *that* far ahead."

Chapter Nine

"DID you have a nice time at the party?" Patsy asked, when they met outside of school on Monday. Her cold had miraculously disappeared, but Jennifer didn't comment.

"Oh, yes, it was super," she declared. "We all missed you, though."

"I'll bet. I'll just bet they all missed me," Patsy said, without rancor.

Jenny flushed. "Well, we did! Especially me." She cast a worried little glance at her friend, disturbed more than she wanted to admit by Patsy's blank expression. It should be so easy to say, "Pat, what's with you and Griff?" But she couldn't. Anyway she couldn't right now, when it was so much more comfortable to just drift along.

Patsy's blue eyes were regarding her solemnly. "Look, Jennifer," she said abruptly. "I guess I owe you an explanation."

And then suddenly Jennifer didn't want to know. She wanted things to go on just as they were. Without any further complications, any conflicting loyalties. She glanced at her watch. "Oh, Pat, I have to scramble. I forgot to copy some notes over the week end and my notebook is all topsy-turvy. See you at lunch. O.K.?" She tossed a smile over her shoulder as she sped away. Patsy looked after her curiously.

In the lunchroom Jenny and Patsy found places at different ends of the long center table. Griff had saved a place for Jenny and he slid over to make room for her.

Just before the bell rang Jennifer glanced at the table near the window and saw Diane Winters watching her. She lifted her hand in a swift, friendly greeting before she thought, Why, just a couple of weeks ago that was me over there. The newcomer, the outsider. And close on the heels of this thought was another. I ought to be the one to make friends with her, make her feel welcome. It would be poetic justice or something. Tomorrow. . . .

Griff had turned his head to see who she was waving at. He looked back at Jennifer slowly. "Well, hey!" he said, in a bright, interested voice. "Who's your friend?"

"That's the cute blonde I was telling you about," a boy across the table said.

"Her name's Diane Winters. She's a new girl, a transfer from some school in California. I'll bet she's lonesome. Why don't we invite her over to this table tomorrow?" Jennifer was speaking just to Griff and hadn't noticed the way everyone had stopped talking to listen. They were all watching her, and she noticed several amused grins as she waited for Griff to answer.

Griff looked uncomfortable and a little annoyed. When the boy across the table murmured, "Yeah, why don't we do that, Griff?" he pretended not to hear.

"On the other hand," a girl broke in sweetly, "why don't we just let sleeping dogs lie?"

The little wave of laughter was terminated by the ringing of the first bell, and benches were pushed back with a sliding, scraping sound that was immediately engulfed in the staccato rhythm of hurrying footsteps and the drone of last-minute snatches of conversation.

Jennifer looked at the retreating backs of her new friends with hurt and resentment in her eyes. "If there's some huge joke going on," she said stiffly, "I'd like to get in on it."

Griff gave her a funny crooked smile. "Don't mind them, Jenny. Just a bunch of comedians."

By the time school was out Jenny had almost forgotten the disturbing episode at the lunch table.

There was a strange car parked in the driveway when she reached home. Even before she walked into the house Jenny knew they had company, but the last thing in the world she expected to see was her mother sitting on the davenport, drinking tea and chatting cozily with Mrs. Kirby—Caroline Kirby, the woman from the Alcoholics Anonymous group back East.

"Oh, hi, darling!" Her mother greeted her brightly. "Caroline and I were just talking about you. You remember Mrs. Kirby, don't you?"

"Yes, of course," Jennifer said, hoping that she didn't sound as dismayed as she was feeling. "How are you, Mrs. Kirby? It's nice to see you again."

"It's nice to see you, Jenny," Mrs. Kirby replied quietly, but her gray eyes saw through the girl's politeness, recognizing and then ignoring the unspoken resentment. "I was just telling your mother I couldn't bear to be within thirty miles of this place and not look you up."

"And you *are* staying for dinner," Jennifer's mother broke in swiftly. "I insist, Caroline, I really do. Why, Chuck would never forgive me if I let you get away before he sees you."

"Well, if you're sure it won't be any bother," Mrs. Kirby began tentatively.

"What do you mean, bother? We have to eat anyway." Jenny's mother got to her feet and smiled down at her friend; then she turned to include Jennifer in her smile. "Honey, look after our guest while I see about whipping up some pies. Having Caroline here certainly calls for some sort of celebration, and I've been hoarding those wild blackberries for just such an occasion."

Her mother headed for the kitchen and there was nothing for Jennifer to do but to sit down and try to make polite conversation.

Jenny said yes, she liked school very much; yes, she'd made a lot of new friends; yes, it certainly was a pretty little town. She asked Mrs. Kirby about her trip. Oh, she flew out? Did she enjoy air travel? Was it a vacation trip or did she intend to make her home in the West?

Mrs. Kirby smiled. "Well, actually I'm combining a business and pleasure trip, Jenny. I'm a delegate to a convention that will be held in Seattle this week end, and since I've always wanted to see this part of the country it seemed a wonderful opportunity to take a winter holiday."

"Oh," Jenny said. "I was just wondering who was . . . you know, minding the store until you got back."

She had only meant to be mildly funny, but she knew at once that her remark had sounded both rude and senseless. "I'm very sorry, Mrs. Kirby," she said slowly. "I guess that wasn't very funny."

"No, it wasn't," Mrs. Kirby agreed, and then softened the words with a smile. "You still resent me, don't you, Jenny? Not just me, but all the things I represent to you. Well, I expect that's natural enough. But your mother doesn't resent us, Jenny. She knows that we're her friends."

"I know. I really am sorry." Jennifer got up stiffly and went to rearrange her books on the desk, to move an ash tray and wipe some nonexistent dust from the table top. When she came back to her place on the davenport she spoke bluntly. "We moved out here so that we could forget all—all the trouble and unhappiness and uncertainty. I'm sorry, but seeing you and talking to you brings it all back. It . . . it scares me, Mrs. Kirby."

The older woman looked at her with pitying eyes. "Why should it scare you, my dear? It doesn't frighten your mother."

"How do you know? How do you know it doesn't make her remember all that—that other?"

Mrs. Kirby continued to regard her calmly. "But, Jenny, how could it make her remember? She's never forgotten."

"Of course she's forgotten. All of us have forgotten," Jenny insisted stubbornly.

Mrs. Kirby shook her head. "No. None of you have really forgotten. You just haven't learned to live with it yet. You're making the same mistake your mother made when she lost Molly. Trying to close a part of your life away from you by pretending that it never happened."

"What do you expect us to do? Broadcast the fact that my mother is a member of Alcoholics Anonymous? Tell everyone about all that time in hospitals and sanatoriums taking cures? Brag about it?"

"Jenny, my poor child." Mrs. Kirby's tone was sorrowful. "Are you still torturing yourself? Still waiting each day for the inevitable recurrence?"

"Of course not." Jenny spoke so shortly that she sounded almost rude. "Of course not," she said again.

Just then her mother called from the kitchen, something about wanting Jenny to go to the store for her. Jenny welcomed the chance to escape.

Mrs. Kirby stayed for dinner, but despite the insistence of both Jennifer's mother and father she refused the offer of making their home her headquarters. "No, I really have to be in Seattle, and the car is supposed to be back by midnight. I'm renting it on a day-to-day basis," she explained.

She stayed until long after Jennifer had excused

herself and gone to her room. Jennifer could hear the voices in the living room for quite a while after she was in bed. But in the morning Mrs. Kirby was gone and everything was back to normal: her father reading the paper while he drank his coffee and had his breakfast, her mother fussing about the small amount Jennifer was eating these days. Mrs. Kirby's unexpected visit might never have happened; on the surface, at least, everything was exactly the same.

They talked about her after Jennifer's father had gone to work and before it was time for Jenny to leave for school. "It was pleasant seeing Caroline again, wasn't it?" her mother asked, and Jennifer mumbled something that passed for assent.

"Will she be coming back, do you suppose?" Jennifer asked carefully, and her mother said with obvious regret that it would probably be impossible for Caroline to spare another day from her crowded schedule.

"How do you suppose she knew where to find us?" Jennifer made herself ask the question, even though she was fairly certain what the answer would be.

"Why, darling, I had sent her our address—told her if she was ever out this way to be sure to look us up."

"Oh." Jennifer spoke briefly. "And those other people, did you give them our address and ask them to look us up too?"

Her mother looked at her in perplexity. "If by

'those other people' you mean my friends back East, yes, I expect I did issue a sort of blanket invitation. Why, Jenny? Do you object?"

"It isn't my business," Jenny said. "It's just that I should think it might be a little awkward for you."

"Awkward in what way, Jenny?"

Jenny waved both hands vaguely. "Well, suppose some of those people do come out here to visit . . . if one of them happened to mention anything about when we lived back East. . . ." She broke off then and stared at her mother, appalled at the look on her mother's white face.

"Well, go on," Mrs. Martin said evenly. "If one of them happened to mention when we lived back East. What then?"

Jennifer pulled her thoughts sharply back into focus. "Nothing," she said. "I don't know why I said that. It doesn't mean anything at all."

Patsy was late that morning, as usual. Jennifer helped her get her locker open and her coat hung up before the first bell rang. She even offered her comb and helped Patsy sort out her books as they hurried along the corridor toward their first class.

"Thanks, Jenny, you're an absolute lifesaver," she panted. "One of these days I'm going to be on time, and the entire student body will drop dead."

"What's the alibi today?" Jennifer asked, and braced herself for another of Patsy's wild yarns. Patsy could always make a good story out of any household calamity. This morning, however, she wasn't her usual exuberant self.

"Oh, no special alibi. Just too much to do and too little time to do it in."

She paused at the door of the classroom and looked at Jennifer soberly. "Look, Jenny, could you come home with me this afternoon? I thought we might do our homework together and maybe have some time to really talk. We never seem to have much time for each other at school nowadays." She didn't say it accusingly, but Jennifer could fill in all the things that Patsy had left unsaid: ever since the business about Griff inviting you to that party you've been avoiding me; you eat your lunch with Griff and half the time he walks home with you; when I call you're usually too busy to talk; and when the other girls are around you're afraid of what they might say about Griff that would embarrass me.

Patsy was waiting for an answer, and for a moment Jennifer toyed with the idea of telling her the exact truth: it isn't that I don't like you as much as ever, Patsy; it's just . . . I'm not comfortable with you because you make me feel disloyal and ashamed of myself. I want to *know* about you and Griff, whether you really like him or not, but I can't ask because I don't want you to tell me.

She looked at Patsy and managed a faint smile. "Why sure, Pat, it sounds like fun. I'll have to call home first and clear it with Mother, but I'm sure she'll be agreeable."

"Oh, swell! I'll meet you at the Coke Bar on the corner and you can call home from there. Be sure to bring your French books. We could both stand some boning up on our phrasing."

"Amen," Jennifer said piously. "Not to mention math and composition and stuff like that."

Patsy giggled. "Well, we can't expect to get all the kinks out in one afternoon, but we can make a start. See you at three-thirty."

The rest of the day Jennifer divided her time between hoping that her mother would let her go and hoping that she wouldn't. The old easiness she had enjoyed with Patsy had been somehow spoiled. Of course, if Patsy had come right out and said that Griff was her dream man, or if Griff had hinted that he had once been interested in Patsy, or if Jennifer had inquired around a little before snapping up Griff's invitation. . . .

But it was certainly too late to worry about all the ifs, Jennifer reminded herself, as the hands of the clock crept closer and closer to three-fifteen.

Chapter Ten

BUT in the end it was surprisingly easy.

She met Patsy at the Coke Bar on the corner, and Patsy waited while Jennifer called home to tell her mother that she was going to do her homework with Pat and might be a little late. Her mother said that would be fine, but her voice sounded odd, and Jennifer felt a sudden little prickling of alarm.

"Mother?" She spoke the word on a sharp upward inflection. "Mother? You're all right, aren't you? Your voice sounds funny, as though you might not be feeling very well."

There was a little silence and then her mother spoke with forced brightness. "I'm fine, Jenny. As a matter of fact, I was just preparing tea for some company. A couple of ladies from the Circle are coming over to talk to me about the plans for our Christmas party."

"Oh, yes, the orphan racket," Jennifer teased her.

"Don't forget to put in our order for that three-year-old girl. Get a blonde, if you can." She was smiling as she hung up the receiver and turned back to Patsy. "It's O.K.," she said. "I can come."

They walked toward Patsy's home slowly, talking about all those unimportant things that are so important at sixteen. About whether the new fad of wearing mismatched socks would really catch on; whether the new teacher would be the colossal bore that his first lecture indicated; whether the Thanksgiving party the parents were planning would be held in the school gym or the ballroom of the hotel.

"Of course the hotel would be a lot more glamorous," Patsy said, "but it costs so much that they'd have to cut down on the refreshments, and the boys would just hate that! Have you ever noticed how important food is to boys?"

Jennifer nodded solemnly. "I suppose it's because they're growing so fast, or something. They need a lot of fuel to keep them going."

"I guess that must be it." Patsy looked at her friend and then hastily transferred her attention to the lavishly autographed jacket of her science book. "Jennifer," she said abruptly, "I suppose you've been wondering what goes with this business about Griff Nolan."

"Yes, I have been wondering. What does go,

Patsy?" She turned her head, but all she could see
was the curve of Patsy's cheek. Patsy was waving to
someone across the block. When she looked back at
Jennifer her eyes were unnaturally bright, but her
voice was exactly the same, not rattled or upset or
anything.

"Griff and I went around together quite a bit last
fall and most of the summer. We weren't going steady
or anything like that, but we went out on a few dates
and to most of the parties." She paused and looked at
Jennifer directly. "Someone must have mentioned
something about it, by now. . . ."

Jennifer shrugged. "Oh, I heard a rumor now and
then. But I didn't pay too much attention. I knew
we'd get around to talking about it sooner or later."
It was funny how easy it was once they had started.
"But . . . you weren't going steady with Griff, you
say?"

"Oh, no. Anyway my mother is dead set against it.
Going steady, I mean. She thinks sixteen is too young.
No . . . as a matter of fact, Griff was going steady
with another girl when I first met him. Norma Willis.
You know Norma, don't you?"

Jennifer nodded. "I think so. A tall blonde girl, sort
of snippy?" She didn't have to wait for Patsy's answering nod. She knew that the girl who had said,
"It figures," when Jennifer admitted being Griff's date

was Norma Willis. Patsy was watching her. Clearly
some sort of response was indicated. "I'm glad you're
telling me about this, Pat," she went on mildly, "because I was a little upset about it. I had the crazy idea
you didn't like it because I was going out with Griff."

There! The words had been uttered and the heav-
ens hadn't fallen. Patsy continued to regard her with
the same half-wistful, half-embarrassed expression.
"Well, I don't exactly like the idea," Patsy said carefully. "Not because of Griff. I honestly don't care
that much about Griff. But because you're my friend,
and because you're so nice."

Jennifer's eyebrows lifted. "And Griff isn't?"

"Oh, he's nice enough . . . I guess," Patsy said a little
doubtfully. "But you can't depend on him, Jenny. For
example, I didn't know that he'd been going steady
with Norma until after he'd been giving me a big rush
for a couple of weeks. Griff never thinks to mention
little items like that. Maybe he just doesn't think
they're important enough, but it can be pretty embarrassing for a girl. You must have heard plenty of hints
about me these past weeks."

"A few," Jennifer admitted.

"The thing is," Patsy rushed on, evidently determined to have the matter cleared up once and for all,
"the thing is that Griff always gives the new girls a
big rush."

"Maybe he's just the fickle type," Jennifer said, and hated the hostile note that had crept unbidden into her voice. "Or maybe he just hasn't met a girl he really likes yet."

"Maybe not," Patsy said cheerfully, and gave Jennifer her old disarming smile. "Maybe that's why he's been playing the field."

After that they stopped talking about Griff. It was ridiculous that Jennifer should feel they were both still thinking about him, even while they discussed what they would wear to the Thanksgiving dance.

When they reached Patsy's house their schoolwork claimed all their attention; there wasn't even time to listen to records, because Jennifer had promised to be home before dark. It was when they were closing their books preparatory to Jennifer's leaving that Patsy said casually, "Hank Bradford asked me to go to the Thanksgiving dance with him. Did I tell you?"

Jennifer looked at her friend searchingly, remembering the hocus-pocus about Patsy's date for the Johnsons' party. "No, you didn't mention it," she said slowly.

Patsy grinned, seeming to read her friend's mind. "I'm telling you the truth this time, Jenny. He really did ask me. That's one good thing about this town— there are quite a lot of nice boys in it." If there was

JENNIFER 139

a gentle note of warning underlying the light words, Jennifer preferred to ignore it.

She walked home through the early dusk, feeling lighthearted and strangely at peace with the world. It was wonderful having the nagging little doubts and resentments brought out into the open. She could plan on the Thanksgiving dance without having to worry about Patsy's hurt feelings and what the others might think. Patsy would be going with Hank Bradford and she would be going with Griff. Maybe they could even double date. That certainly ought to quell any rumors about Griff's spoiling their friendship.

When she reached home she saw that the ladies from the Circle were still there, and ran into the house eagerly to meet them. Her mother was always so proud to introduce Jenny to these new friends of hers. The moment she entered the house, however, she knew that something was wrong. She knew it! It was something she could feel like a draft blowing across her neck, feathering fear along her spine.

Her mother sat stiffly on the very edge of her chair, facing the two women on the davenport. They were all balancing their teacups carefully, but the faces that turned when Jennifer came to the doorway were polite frozen faces. Her mother's smile was a mask that didn't quite hide the bleakness in her eyes. She gave Jennifer a quick nod.

Jenny realized vaguely that she ought to know one of the women. She had called at the house several times on business about the Circle.

"Well, hello," Jennifer said, and waited for her mother to cue her. Usually her mother was very sharp about things like that. Jenny dear, you remember Mrs. Hartman, or Wilson—or whatever the woman's name was. So that Jenny could say, "Of course I remember. How are you, Mrs. So-and-so?"

But this time her mother just gave her a dazed look and then said, "Hello, Jenny. Would you see about getting the potatoes on? It's fearfully late."

Jennifer almost gasped, because it was so rude, so completely unlike her mother to be practically pushing these women out of the house, implying that it was almost dinnertime.

The strange woman was looking at Jennifer coldly. "This is your daughter, Mrs. Martin?"

"Yes. My daughter Jennifer. Jennifer, Mrs. Copeland and Mrs. Roberts." Her mother recited the names woodenly.

What could be the matter with Mother?

"Mrs. Copeland," Jennifer repeated with a smile. "And of course I've met Mrs. Roberts. It's nice to see you again, Mrs. Roberts."

Mrs. Roberts immediately became very busy gathering up her purse and gloves, stuffing letters back into her purse, glancing at her wrist watch. "It really is getting very late and we should be getting along." She looked at the other woman as if for help, and Mrs. Copeland stepped into the pause resolutely. Whatever the situation was, you could see that Mrs. Copeland was enjoying it. There was a shine in her beady eyes that reminded Jennifer of a cat stalking a wounded bird, and she knew instantly that here was someone she could learn to hate without the slightest effort.

She put her schoolbooks down and crossed the room to perch on the arm of her mother's chair. It was an automatic defensive reflex, but her mother didn't even seem to know she was there. Her stiff figure didn't relax at all.

"I wish you'd see about those potatoes, Jenny," she said again.

Mrs. Copeland rose to her feet majestically. "You understand that there isn't anything personal in this, Mrs. Martin. It's just that we have an obligation to these children and must do what we think best for them."

"Of course."

"And we hope you'll continue to come to the meetings," Mrs. Roberts burst in. "We've all enjoyed having you in the Circle."

"Thank you."

It was evident to Jenny by this time that her mother was not being deliberately rude and ungracious. She was behaving exactly like a sleepwalker.

"And of course I don't have to assure you that this information will go no further," Mrs. Copeland purred. "We aren't trying to make trouble. We're simply trying to fulfill an obligation."

"To the children," Jennifer's mother interrupted, and this time there could be no doubt that the rudeness was intentional. "Yes, you've pointed that out several times."

"Well, really. . . ." Mrs. Copeland started to bristle and then changed her mind. She turned instead to the other woman. "Come, Helene, we must be going." She didn't offer to shake hands and she didn't thank Jennifer's mother for the tea, although her mother's prized silver tea service and a plate of cookies were still on the table.

Mrs. Roberts did offer her hand and after a barely perceptible pause Jennifer's mother accepted it limply.

"You will come to our meetings, won't you?" Mrs. Roberts was trying valiantly to preserve a friendly note for the moment of parting. "The first Thursday of the month. We'll be expecting you."

"Thank you," Jennifer's mother said again.

When the door had closed behind the two women, Jennifer started gathering up the tea things. She carried them out into the kitchen and stacked them neatly on the drainboard. After that, she put away her school coat and piled the books on the desk. Her mother said nothing, nothing at all. She stood beside the window, looking out at the place where the women's car had been parked near the curb.

Jennifer hesitated and then went and stood very close beside her. After a moment her mother turned her head and spoke. "Well," she said flatly, "that is that."

"What is what?" Jennifer asked. "And who was that unpleasant woman? She had a face that would look well on a totem pole, maybe, but it certainly didn't do anything for *her!*"

"Mrs. Copeland is one of the trustees at the Orphans' Home," Jennifer's mother said. "Our application was turned down, Jenny. We can't have one of the children for Christmas."

"Why not?" Jennifer asked, knowing suddenly exactly why not, but hoping desperately that her mother would offer some other reason, any other reason.

Her mother went back to the davenport and sat down. "We had to have some references, people who had known us for at least five years. I thought about Mr. Phillips. You remember the man your father used to work for back East? Unfortunately, his wife opened the letter and took it upon herself to answer it."

Jennifer's eyes darkened but she said nothing. She remembered Mrs. Phillips, all right—a prim, domineering woman with cold brown eyes and a rigid disciplined mouth. The type, Jennifer told herself, who *would* open mail addressed to her husband.

Jennifer's mother laughed suddenly, a laugh that should have been amused and wasn't; a laugh that tried to say she didn't care. "You should have heard that letter, Jenny. It really was a masterpiece. She must have toiled over it. She called herself a God-fearing woman. 'I am a God-fearing woman, Mrs. Copeland,' she said, 'a church-going woman, and I am appalled, simply appalled at the idea of turning an innocent child over to the custody of a woman like Mrs. Charles G. Martin!' She wanted to be sure the committee would know she was referring to the same Mrs. Martin they were investigating."

"What committee?" Jennifer asked faintly.

Her mother shrugged, as if the matter were really of no importance. "Three or four of the women from the Circle, and some of the trustees from the Orphans' Home. These two were just the—the advance guard. By now the story should be all over town. The letter came this morning."

"They said that the—the information wouldn't go any further," Jenny reminded her soberly.

Her mother smiled sadly. "Oh, come now, Jenny," she said.

"The old . . . busybodies!" Jennifer said, with sudden anger in her voice. "The old troublemakers! I wish I'd been home. I'd have slammed the door in their smug, pious faces. I'd have ordered them out of the house, that's what I'd have done."

"No." Her mother spoke quietly. "No. It was bound to happen sooner or later. At least now it's *happened* and we don't have to worry about it any more."

Jennifer stared. Why, Mrs. Kirby was right. Mother hadn't forgotten; she hadn't forgotten any of it. Jennifer wasn't the only one who had been terrified every day that the past might reach out and touch them, might throw a faint but unmistakable shadow across their paths, might hold the sword of Damocles over their heads.

"I really should have asked Mrs. Copeland if I might keep Mrs. Phillips' letter," Jennifer's mother went on mildly. "I had no idea that she kept such good track of me. It was all there, Jenny—names, dates, places—everything. She knew exactly how much time I'd spent in the sanatorium; she even had the release date. And she told them all about the time I'd been picked up by the police as an amnesia victim."

"She was always a hateful woman," Jennifer said stonily. "I always felt sorry for poor Mr. Phillips."

"So did I," her mother said, with a ghost of her old smile. "God-fearing or not, Mrs. Phillips must be a most uncomfortable person to live with." She got up from the davenport and moved toward the kitchen, but slowly, as if she were suddenly very tired. "I suppose we should be thinking about getting dinner on the table. It's almost time for your father to be home." Jennifer followed her, shaken with pity, not knowing how to express it, not really wanting to express it.

Her father sensed at once that something was wrong. Jenny wished there was some way she might have warned him, might have turned aside the questions, but she couldn't think of anything. She had to sit at the table and listen while her mother told him of the day's events in a carefully bright tone that insisted they were quite unimportant.

Her father accepted the whole thing casually, a little too casually to be entirely convincing. "So a bunch of the old hens will get together and gossip," he said. "So what? Let them! As long as they're talking about us they're giving someone else a rest." A little later he mentioned that one of the men from the plant had invited them over for an evening of bridge. "I told him that we'd be happy to come, Nan. It seemed like a good way to get acquainted. There will be four or five other couples, mostly from around the neighborhood.

Seems that this fellow's wife belongs to some club of yours. Frazier, her name is. Mrs. Lloyd Frazier."

Jennifer watched her mother's fingers tighten around her fork. She didn't speak for a moment, and when her husband looked up at her inquiringly she gave a nervous sort of smile. "But . . . Chuck, do you suppose we should? I mean, wouldn't it just be better to decline with thanks?"

He looked across the table at her gravely. "Because of that business this afternoon, you mean?"

She swallowed. "Yes."

He put down his fork, lining it up with his plate carefully, speaking in the reasonable tone one might use to a recalcitrant child. "Nan, this is our home, this is our town, these are our friends."

"Our friends?" The bitter note was understandable, but it hurt Jennifer to have her mother look like that. "They probably just want to look us over." Her eyes were flashing but her face was pale. "Can't you just imagine how the phones must have been ringing all day, Chuck? I can. And I'm not going to walk into anything so unpleasant. I'm not going to let *you* walk into anything so unpleasant."

"Not even if I want to?"

"Why should you want to?" She hurled the words at him.

"Because one of the things you have never been,

Nan, is a coward. You're honest, and because you're honest you're going to accept the fact that there will be talk. Maybe some of them will even turn up their noses. But all the things they talk about are long ago and far away. This is here and now. Nothing they say can hurt us if we don't let it hurt us."

Jennifer's mother was silent for a long moment and then she looked at Jennifer.

"Yes, why don't you go, Mother?" Jenny said. "You don't have to worry about the dishes. I'll whip them up after you've gone."

But Mrs. Martin continued to sit there, looking from her child to her husband with tormented eyes. "You just don't know," she said at last. "You haven't any idea. Mrs. Roberts called right after noon, terribly upset. She wanted to bring one of the trustees from the Orphanage Board over to have a confidential talk with me. She stressed that word 'confidential,' but they probably stopped at half a dozen places on the way over here. They didn't come until after three-thirty."

So that was why she had been so upset when Jenny called about going to Patsy's house to study. Poor Mother, how she must have suffered all afternoon, waiting for them to come and explode the carefully laid foundation of this new life.

"Jenny could invite Pat to come over and stay with

her," Jennifer's father said, just as if the matter were settled. "We probably won't be very late."

"Oh, don't worry about me," Jenny said lightly. "I'm not an infant, you know. I'll do my homework and watch television and go to bed like a good girl about ten-thirty."

Still her mother sat there without moving. Her husband leaned over and covered the hand that was lying listlessly on the white tablecloth. "Please, Nan! Just for me!"

Her mother's eyes never wavered, and suddenly her face changed. Suddenly her whole expression was different—the fear and the uncertainty were gone. "Why, of course you're right, Chuck," she said. "Of course I'll go."

Chapter Eleven

JENNIFER was sound asleep when her parents came home. She didn't even hear the car drive in, but she wakened in the morning to a heartening sound. Her mother was humming as she moved about the kitchen, putting the coffee to perk, plugging in the toaster, and setting the table.

Jennifer scrambled into her clothes in record time and hurried out to join her parents at the breakfast table. "Did you have a good time last night?" she asked cautiously, as she slid into her place at the table. Her father grunted assent without lifting his eyes from the paper, but Jennifer's mother gave her a serene smile.

"Yes, it was very pleasant. You know me and bridge!" She made a self-depreciating little face. "But at least I didn't make any glaring errors. They want us to come again." She went about pouring the coffee and filling the fruit-juice glasses just as if she were reporting a perfectly ordinary evening.

Maybe it will be all right, Jennifer thought, remembering the new expression she had seen on her mother's face the evening before. Then she changed the thought. I just know it's going to be all right now, she said to herself.

Presently Mr. Martin pushed back his chair and got to his feet. After he had kissed Jennifer and her mother, he got his overcoat from the hall closet, located his brief case, and went off whistling to get the car out of the garage.

The kitchen was quiet after he had gone. Jennifer and her mother divided the morning paper and Jennifer finished her breakfast while her mother had another cup of coffee. Much as she wanted to hear about last evening, Jennifer couldn't quite bring herself to ask any more questions. Were they really nice, Mother? she wanted to say. Did you have the feeling that you were on exhibition? Did anyone say anything at all about the orphans, or about Mrs. Copeland?

When they traded papers her mother spoke quietly. "It really was a nice evening. Mrs. Frazier was so pleasant. I had the feeling that she knew about the letter Mrs. Copeland had received but was willing to believe all that Mrs. Phillips wrote was over and done with now."

Jennifer watched her mother's face as she talked. There were probably other things that her mother wasn't telling about—barbed remarks and sly little smiles. But last night's look of calm and determination was still there. Suddenly Jennifer glowed with pride in her mother! She has done what Mrs. Kirby said, she thought. Mother has won her battle! She's not afraid any more! She wished she had the words to tell her all that she was thinking, all that she was feeling. But words were such clumsy things. So often when you tried to tell a person something it was better to choose a roundabout way.

"You're very quiet this morning," her mother said, after a long silence.

Then suddenly Jenny knew just the right words to say—words that would tell her mother that she, too, was unafraid and confident about the future. "It sounds silly, I know," she said slowly, "but I was wondering how to ask you if I could give a party."

"A party?" her mother repeated the word doubtfully. "You want to give a party, Jennifer? Here?"

"Yes. Not right away, of course, but maybe around the Thanksgiving holiday. I've met so many of the kids now, and I went to that party at the Johnsons' and several times I've visited at Elsie's or Pat's house.

It just seemed like a good time to get the whole gang together at our house. It's such a lovely house for a party."

She said it matter-of-factly, just as if her mother hadn't been wanting her to invite her friends to her home, just as if her father hadn't urged her to start building a carefree life for herself, just as if fear had not been holding her back.

That fear had begun on her ninth birthday.

She had hurried home from school so eagerly that afternoon. She was going to change into her best dress and her new shoes and be all ready to meet her small guests at the door.

She was smiling to herself as she skipped happily along the last long block. She wouldn't even ask anyone if they had brought a present, she vowed blissfully. She would just invite them in and introduce them to her mother and then take them into her own room to put away their coats. Afterwards they would play games like musical chairs or pin-the-tail-on-the-donkey. There would be prizes and party favors and ice cream and cake with thick pink icing. She would sit at the head of the table and when she opened the presents she would thank everyone nicely.

But it didn't happen that way at all. It was her father who opened the door to her cheerful banging.

He explained quietly that her mother was ill and there could be no party, but on Saturday he would take all the children to a matinee instead. How would that be?

Jennifer had been heartbroken and unexpectedly rebellious. "Mother's always sick when I want to do something special. She won't go to PTA or to the school concerts or anything. She won't even go to the Girl Scout meetings or the bake sales at church. Charleen's mother says that my mother isn't even sick at all. She says that Mother is just plain—"

But her father had grabbed her shoulders and given her a hard shake and Jennifer had never uttered the frightening word except to herself.

Jennifer couldn't face her friends, who had been talking all day about the birthday party and hinting at what presents they were bringing her. She went in and threw herself across her bed, and every time the doorbell rang she held her hands over her ears to shut out the sound of her father's voice explaining and explaining.

Her father did take them to the matinee on Saturday, just as he had promised, and afterwards he marched the ten little girls into a wonderful soda fountain and bought them all lavish ice-cream sundaes and little pink cakes. But it wasn't the same, it wasn't the same at all.

All the girls said it was a wonderful party, the best one ever, but even that didn't make it right. Not even when her mother bought her the new doll with real hair and magic skin and eyes that opened and closed, not even when she held Jennifer on her lap and rocked her back and forth and said, "I'm sorry. Mother's so sorry, baby. It will never happen again, I promise you."

There had been no more plans for parties after that.

Now her mother gave her a smile. "Why, a holiday party sounds wonderful, Jenny. We'll start making plans right away. How many will there be, do you suppose?"

"Well, I'm not sure. I'll have to think about it some more. Mike had about twenty at his place, I think."

It wasn't time to leave for school yet, so they made a few tentative plans while Jennifer stacked the dishes.

"We'll just let them build their own sandwiches," Jenny's mother said. "Lots of cold meats and pickles and olives and potato chips and tomato wedges. . . ."

"And cheese," Jennifer reminded her. "Griff's crazy about cheese."

"Cheese, by all means," her mother said, smiling. "And lots of Coke."

"It sounds dreamy already," Jennifer declared, and

then glanced at her watch and snatched the books off the corner of the table. "My goodness, I have to fly! We'll talk about it some more tonight. O.K.?"

"O.K., darling."

Jennifer's swift kiss slid along her mother's cheek. "Thanks, Mother," she said, and her voice was just a little huskier than usual.

She hurried down the walk, and then stopped for a moment to fling one arm dramatically around the tree that stood on the parking strip. "I love you," she whispered against the cool bark. "And now we've got roots here too. I think everything is all right."

A cheerful voice hailed her before she could move away. Elsie and Bill were running along the sidewalk toward her, and Jennifer knew that Bill would tell the story all over school. He did, too, right in front of Jennifer. "Hey, kids, Jenny kisses her tree good-by before she comes to school. How about that?"

"I don't see anything peculiar about it," Jennifer protested. "That tree is a member of the family. Like a cousin or an aunt or something. . . ."

Laughter exploded around her, but it was friendly laughter.

A tall boy walking past looked at the group clustered about Jennifer, and she thought there was a hint of envy in his smile. He didn't stop, though, even when one of the boys yelled, "Hi, Ed!" He just lifted his hand in a friendly manner and kept right on going.

That evening Griff took her to a movie and then came home and watched her fix hot chocolate and cinnamon toast. A few days later he came over and helped her with her homework, and once when some of the others were going dancing he called at the last minute and asked Jennifer if she wanted to go. It was almost the same as going steady. Griff just naturally dropped into the place next to her at the lunch table, and he often walked home with her, letting her carry his books, just for a gag.

Jennifer planned to tell Griff about her party before she mentioned it to the others, but somehow she never did.

One day when she was starting down to the lunchroom she ran into Diane Winters and, without even stopping to think about it, invited Diane to sit with her at the big center table.

Diane looked pleased. "Why . . . thanks, I'd love to. I was hoping someone would ask me. You always seem to be having such a good time at your table."

If anyone was surprised when the two girls came in together no one mentioned it. Jennifer was aware of a few quickly covered grins and Norma Willis looked quickly from Jennifer to Griff and then back at Jennifer again.

"Hi, everyone! This is Diane Winters." She made

the introduction casually and then waited for someone to move over and make room for her and Diane.
Griff slid along the bench, leaving just enough room
so that one of the girls could sit on each side of him.

When they had taken their places, Griff gave Diane
his big grin, the grin that seemed shy until you knew
Griff. "This is the way I like to have things work out,"
he said. "A rose between two thorns."

Diane giggled. She had a cute little giggle, like a
child's. She had a dimple, too, Jennifer noticed dis-
passionately, and wondered if Griff liked girls with
dimples.

When she looked up and down the table for Patsy,
someone volunteered that Pat had a bad cold and
had asked for an early-dismissal slip.

"Oh, dear," Jennifer said. "I wanted to tell her about
my party."

Ears pricked up at the mention of a party. You
could almost see them prick up. "What party, Jennifer?"

"Mine," she said complacently. "Mother said I
could throw a real wing-ding to celebrate getting settled in this lovely school and meeting such a lovely
group of children." She slanted a quick grin around
the table as she spoke, and dropped her eyes demurely
when a chorus of groans greeted this announcement.

"Lovely group of children!" One of the boys echoed

her words in a hollow voice. "Oh, boy, I can see it now. Ice cream and cake and funny hats and probably pin-the-tail-on-the-donkey."

"Probably," Jennifer said. "But the menu is going to be just build-yourself sandwiches and Cokes and potato chips and cheese." She smiled at Griff. "And maybe ice-cream sundaes for dessert if the budget can stand it." She went on eating her lunch, but pretty soon she thought of something else and leaned across Griff to speak to Diane. "You're invited too, Diane. It will give you a chance to meet all the kids."

"It sounds dreamy," Diane said. "Can I bring my brother? Ed doesn't know anyone either, except for the boys he plays basketball with."

Griff looked up quickly. "Ed? Oh, sure—Ed Winters. Naturally he'd be your brother. I catch on quick."

The others took up the chant. "Ed? Oh, yes. Sort of tall and easygoing." "He's in one of my classes." "He's a doll." One of the girls contributed this last.

"Did I ever meet him?" Jennifer asked. "I mean, I can't remember a new boy." She was looking around the lunchroom as she spoke. "Doesn't your brother eat lunch?" she asked Diane.

"He works during his lunch hour and after school, too, at that service station on the corner," Diane explained without embarrassment. "You must have seen him around, though, Jennifer. Anyway, he's seen you."

"He has?" Jennifer looked properly mystified, but she couldn't help being pleased at the way the conversation was going. It certainly wasn't going to hurt anything to have Griff realize that other boys noticed her.

Diane was nodding. "Oh, yes. I was telling Ed about you that first day, about how you helped me with my locker. And he said, 'Oh, sure. The cute little gal in brown with the black-and-white convertible.'"

There was a hoot of laughter and a series of quickly smothered chuckles. "Now don't tell us you're being loved for your car alone, Jennifer," someone heckled.

"Well, I *hope* not," Jennifer said with complete good nature. "After all, it isn't even my own car!"

"Little brown gal, hmm?" That was Bill and his eyes were bright with mischief. "Yep, it suits you, Jenny. Brown eyes, brown hair, brown sweater. Sort of smoky eyelashes."

Griff, who had helped himself to one of Diane's sandwiches, divided a quick smile between the two girls. "This gives me a fascinating idea," he said. "Since Diane's a stranger in town, why don't I take her to your party, Jennifer?"

For a moment Jennifer felt as though she couldn't possibly say a word. Then she reached over and took a pear, bit into it, and nodded. "O.K. by me," she said.

"But I was kind of counting on you, Griff, to help with the party."

"Oh, sure, I'll be glad to help," Griff answered carelessly. "But that won't stop me from escorting this glamour gal here. How about it, Beautiful?"

There was complete silence in the room, as everyone waited to see what would happen. Jennifer could feel all the curious eyes on her face. She managed to go on eating, although it was hard to force the food past the hurting place in her chest. Her smile felt stiff, but if anyone suspected that she was shaking inside there was no outward indication.

If I can just get through these next few minutes, she thought frantically. If I can just hold out until the bell rings! If I can just get through my next class without breaking down!

It went on like that for the rest of the interminable day. Her eyes smarted with the tears that crowded behind her eyelids, her throat hurt, and there was a curious aching spot in her chest.

She hurried to her locker as soon as the bell rang, but even though she hurled her things into place Diane Winters was there before she could escape.

"Oh, hi!" Jennifer said, straightening up as the other girl hailed her joyously.

"Thanks a lot for inviting me to sit with you today, Jennifer, and for inviting me to your party." Diane's eyes were shining as she spoke. She really *was* a pretty girl. Nice, too, and it certainly wasn't her fault that Griff had a wandering eye.

"I was wondering if you'd have time to stop and have a Coke with me," Diane went on artlessly. "I haven't felt that I knew any of the girls well enough to ask them, until now."

"I'd love to," Jennifer said promptly. "But I promised my mother I'd come straight home this afternoon. Let me take a rain check, will you?"

It would probably have been just as well to accept her invitation, Jennifer told herself grimly as she hurried toward home, but she couldn't. She simply couldn't sit at the Coke Bar this afternoon and exchange polite chitchat with Diane Winters.

Chapter Twelve

SHE managed somehow to get through the next few days. The week end was a welcome reprieve. It meant that she didn't have a full-time job of pretending that nothing was the matter, pretending that she didn't even notice that Griff sat beside Diane in the lunchroom and waited to walk home with her after school. Not that he wasn't pleasant to Jennifer—he was. He acted as if they were still the best of friends.

The hardest thing of all was to ignore the curious or amused or pitying glances of the other boys and girls. Though she was determined not to see them, Jennifer was perfectly aware that they followed her all through the day—in the classrooms, the lunchroom, after school.

One noon she was sitting next to Patsy in the lunchroom, fighting to control the lump in her throat. Griff sat next to Diane at the other end of the table. Suddenly a new and startling idea came to Jennifer, exploding like a bombshell in her mind. But this is exactly the kind of thing Mother has had to bear! For ages she has had to pretend not to see people when they smiled or looked pityingly at her. She remembered her mother's newly acquired calm and courage. Well, if she can do it, so can I, Jennifer told herself firmly. From that moment on everything became easier.

Diane herself continued to be as friendly as a new puppy, and just as hard to snub. She seemed to *like* Jennifer so well. One day when they were changing classes she confided to Jennifer that Griff wanted to come over and meet her mother. "He's nice, isn't he, Jennifer? Even if he is a little shy."

"Oh, Griff's a living doll," she managed to say lightly.

It was perfectly understandable now why the others had not warned her about Griff. What could they have said? What could she say now to warn Diane?

Griff isn't dependable.

Griff has a roving eye.

Griff always gives the new girls a big rush.

But those were almost word for word the things that Patsy had tried to tell her. Jennifer's face felt hot whenever she remembered how she had turned aside Patsy's tactfully worded warnings. "Maybe Griff has never met the right girl. Maybe that's why he's fickle," she had said.

She was committed to the party. She couldn't have managed to get out of it now even if she had wanted to. Her mother and father were so delighted to help make plans. Her father was even getting a juke-box; some man at the plant was letting him take one from the company's recreation room, a real jukebox with colored lights and a fantastic selection of new records.

She couldn't have called off the party, even without her parents' enthusiasm for the idea. All the boys and girls were talking about it. As if the party had become public property, they all insisted on helping to make plans; it was half the fun.

In spite of herself, Jennifer looked forward to the date, which had been set for one of the last Saturdays in November. It was impossible not to share Patsy's enthusiasm. It was difficult to avoid Diane's gratitude.

One afternoon she found Diane waiting for her beside the lockers when she went to get her coat after school. "Jennifer," Diane began resolutely, "this is pretty embarrassing, but I have to talk to you about y-y-your party." Diane had a little stutter when she was nervous or upset, and it was perfectly clear to Jennifer that she was upset now.

Jennifer waited. Her faintly raised eyebrows and bland smile gave no indication of the way her heart had pounded as she braced herself for the questions Diane was sure to ask.

"What about the party, Diane?" she asked calmly enough.

"Well . . . you see, I seem to have a p-p-positive knack for rushing in where angels fear to tread. And now I j-j-just don't know what to do."

"Since I can't figure out what the big problem is, I don't see how I can help," Jennifer said gravely. "Why don't I just cash in on that rain check? You can buy me a Coke while you confess all."

They went down to the Coke Bar and sat side by side on tall stools while Diane explained between hurried sips of her Coke. "Like a fool I rushed right home and told Ed about your party and how he was going to be invited. You really did say that you were going to ask him, Jennifer, and how could I know you were just kidding?"

"I wasn't kidding," Jennifer said. "I'd really like to have your brother come."

"You aren't saying that just to be polite?"

"Of course not," Jennifer said airily. "I'm never polite."

"Because . . . well, I know he *wants* to come, b-b-but

he wouldn't crash in on just my invitation." The blue eyes were so anguished that Jennifer had to smile.

"Wait! Hold on!" Jennifer interrupted. "You want me to invite him, isn't that it? Well, for goodness' sake, I'll ask him right away! Today, even."

"Oh, Jennifer, would you?" It was impossible to mistake the undisguised relief in Diane's voice, in her eyes. "We could just sort of casually stroll by the service station and I could just sort of casually say, 'Ed, you know Jennifer Martin, don't you?' and then you could. . . ."

"Just sort of casually invite him to the party," Jennifer finished gravely. "O.K. Finish your Coke and we'll do it."

Patsy came in before they had finished their Cokes, and Jennifer outlined the plan for her. "Come along and lend us moral support," she commanded. "It's the least you can do for the party."

They walked past the service station, and there was Ed pumping gas and washing windshields and checking oil. Jennifer realized, as they waited for him to finish with his last customer, that she had seen Ed before. She had passed him a dozen times in the halls, and they had a study period together. Once she had almost tripped over his feet as she hurried toward the library at the end of a period.

The thing was, that Ed didn't make an indelible impression on people; he looked just about like a million other boys. He was tall and pleasant-looking and had nice hair and gray eyes and a quick smile. But he just didn't register. At least he didn't register with Jennifer. When he came over to talk to them she couldn't help seeing that he was embarrassed too, and that made it a little easier.

"Hello, Sis. Hi, Jennifer, Patsy!" He took off his cap and stood turning it between his fingers. The gray eyes were questioning and a little wary.

"I came to invite you to my party," Jennifer said without preamble. "Officially, that is. Diane seemed to feel that secondhand invitations didn't count."

Ed flushed right up to his hairline. "I hope this sister of mine hasn't been twisting your arm," he said uncomfortably.

"Oh, she hasn't," Jennifer assured him quickly. "She simply happened to be an innocent bystander when we were cooking up this plot. The party's next Saturday. I—I hope you'll come, Ed."

"I'd like to," he said. "But I'll have to see about getting time off. Usually I work on Saturdays until about nine-thirty."

Another car drove into the station, and Ed excused himself and hurried off. There didn't seem to be anything to wait for, but they waited anyway. Ed was smiling when he came back to them. "Thanks for the invitation, Jennifer—in case I forgot to say thanks before."

"He's nice," Patsy said firmly, as the three girls walked on up the street. "I like your brother, Diane."

"He really is a swell guy," Diane said. "I don't know how Mother and I would get along without him. He's been the man of the house ever since my father died seven years ago. When he was too small to have a regular job he used to deliver papers." She broke off self-consciously and then smiled at the other two girls. "I hate to sound like I'm trying to sell him, b-b-but that's the reason I'm so anxious for him to g-g-get to know the other kids and have a good time."

"Say no more," Patsy said largely. "Anyway, Ed's attractive enough to get along without a build-up."

Jennifer looked at her friend and nodded. But she couldn't help wondering whether Patsy was just saying the tactful thing or whether she did really think Ed was attractive.

That night when Jennifer's mother suggested that she invite Griff over to help choose the records they wanted on the jukebox, Jennifer had to tell her. "Griff has another girl, Mother. Didn't I tell you about that?"

It was a ridiculous way to say it. Of course she hadn't told her mother. She had done everything possible to keep from admitting it to herself. Aware of her mother's watchful eyes, she tried to give a light laugh, but it didn't come out too well. It broke off in the middle, on a sound like a hiccup. "He's coming to the party, though! He's bringing Diane. After all, it doesn't make a speck of difference if these things don't come out even. There were two extra girls at Mike's party." She went on chattering, just as if it didn't matter at all; but her mother grew more and more quiet. "Anyway, Diane's brother is coming. You'll like him, Mother. He's the boy who works odd hours at the service station just across from school. His name's Ed."

Her father hadn't taken any interest in the conversation up to this point. He had been just wandering around the kitchen while Jennifer and her mother cleared up the dishes. "Ed? Oh, sure! The kid at Joe's Service Station. Nice boy. So he's coming to the party too. Does he go to your school, Jenny?"

"Yes. Ed and his sister just moved here from California. They both seem awfully nice, but Ed's always working and doesn't have much time for fun. Diane says he's been the man of the house for seven years. That's pretty sad, don't you think?"

Her father grinned. "Horatio Alger up to date, eh? But a little honest work never hurt anyone, Jenny.

He'll be better off for learning that early in life."

Later in the evening Patsy came over, and the two girls spent a couple of hours going over the record list and talking about the party. Elsie was supposed to come too, but at the last minute her mother said no, because she hadn't finished her homework.

"If I'd known Elsie couldn't come I'd have asked Norma Willis," Jennifer murmured. "Have you noticed how friendly she's been lately? Ever since. . . ." She stopped, and Patsy looked at her with a faint smile.

"Yes?" she said. "Ever since when?"

Jennifer made a little face. "Ever since I brought Diane over and introduced her to the gang. I guess . . . ever since Griff stopped coming around."

The smile grew a little broader. "Well, now you belong to the club," Patsy explained. "Now you're really one of us—the ex-Griff girls." She put her elbows on the table and rested her chin against her clasped hands. "Come to think of it, we ought to wear some sort of a pin—you know, like sorority sisters."

It was hard to smile in return, hard to change the subject and talk about something else, but Jennifer was learning . . . she was learning.

Her mother was very quiet after Patsy had gone, and it seemed to Jennifer that there was a sad look in her eyes when she kissed her good night. Jenny was still troubled about it long after she was in bed. It wasn't like Mother to be so—so unresponsive. It would have been a lot more natural if her mother had been a little angry about Griff. "Who does he think he is?" That was the attitude her daughter had subconsciously expected her to take. "We'll show that Griff Nolan!" But her mother had said nothing, absolutely nothing. Her eyes had just looked as if it was her fault, or something.

Jennifer stared into the darkness, feeling lost and lonely. The tears that had been dammed up for the last week were slipping slowly down her cheeks. She couldn't help remembering the night Griff had walked her home from the party: the way he had smiled down at her and told her that her hand felt like a puppy's paw, the way he had kissed her good night twice— once for good night and once because she hadn't been mad.

"Griff was so special." She whispered the words sadly, because she realized all at once that she was using the past tense.

Her mother tiptoed into the room just as Jennifer was falling asleep. The hall light was on, and she couldn't help seeing the path of tears along Jennifer's cheek. For a moment she just stood there. Then she leaned forward and smoothed back a lock of hair that had fallen across Jennifer's forehead, her lips moved lightly across Jennifer's cheek, and her whisper was so soft that even if Jennifer had been wide awake she might have missed the words. "I'm so sorry, darling. Mother's so sorry."

The familiar words, so softly spoken, seemed to echo and re-echo in Jennifer's troubled dreams. "Mother's so sorry. . . . Mother's so sorry." And her mother really had been sorry all those other times; she really had intended to be different. But something had always happened to make her forget her promise.

"After that there is nothing to do but start over," Mrs. Kirby said in the dream. "Start over . . . start over . . . start over."

"What are you doing in my dream?" Jennifer asked crossly.

"I want to tell you a story," Mrs. Kirby said, "about a woman named Caroline."

"I've already heard that story," Jennifer interrupted rudely. "And anyway I haven't time to listen. I have to get ready for the party. I'm going to have a party with ice cream and cake with pink icing and pin-the-tail-on-the-donkey."

"No, you aren't," Mrs. Kirby told her sadly. "Your

father will take you to a matinee instead. And your mother will be so sorry . . . so sorry, because no one will come to your party."

"No!" Jennifer shouted. "No . . . no!"

She sat straight up in bed and realized at the same moment that she had shouted out loud. She sat clutching the blanket to her chest while she heard her mother hurrying along the hall, clicking on the lights. When she turned on Jennifer's light, Jennifer stared at her across the room and then said in a shaking voice, "I'm sorry. I guess I had a nightmare."

"Are you all right now? Do you want me to leave the light on for a while?" She wasn't even smiling at the idea of a big girl like Jennifer having nightmares.

"No, I'll be all right now." Jennifer squirmed back into the pillows and gave her mother a tremulous grin. "I dreamed that no one came to my party," she explained. "Did you ever hear of anything so—so silly?"

Her mother didn't say it was silly. She didn't say anything. She just came over and tucked Jennifer in and patted her cheek. Then she turned and went back to her own room.

Jennifer couldn't rid herself of the nagging feeling that her mother was blaming herself, blaming herself because Griff had found another girl. But how could she think that? And then, just before sleep came, the answer occurred to her. Her mother believed that Griff had heard the gossip and had been influenced by it! Her mother, who held her head so high and ignored barbed remarks and sly glances, could be indifferent to public opinion only when it touched herself. She couldn't bear the thought of having it hurt Jenny.

I'll tell her tomorrow, Jennifer promised herself drowsily. I'll make her see that she didn't have a thing to do with it, that Griff always gives the new girls a big rush.

But in the morning she couldn't remember what it was she had meant to tell her mother.

She wakened to the frosty promise of another beautiful day. Her heart was light as she dressed and hurried through her breakfast. She talked so much at the breakfast table that her mother had to remind her that she mustn't be late for school.

Jennifer looked at the kitchen clock and then at the calendar. She gave a little bounce that was one part impatience and two parts excitement. "Just think! Tomorrow's my party! All of a sudden I'm all excited about it. You know—like when you've thought about something for so long you're almost tired of it and then, bang, it's there and even more fun than you'd imagined."

Her father grinned at her over the top of his paper. "Big doings, hmm?"

"Oh, yes. Everyone says it'll be a marvelous party."

Just before she dashed off for school she paused in the doorway and looked back at her mother. "I have a queer feeling that I'm forgetting something. Is there something I was supposed to do, or someone I'm supposed to call?"

Her mother looked back at her gravely. "Nothing I can think of, Jennifer."

"Well, I'll probably think of it later on. It couldn't have been very important." Jennifer glanced over her shoulder, saw that Elsie was coming along the street, and blew her mother an airy kiss. "So long, sweetie! I'll be seeing you."

Chapter Thirteen

AND then suddenly it was The Day.

Jennifer had an appointment to have her hair done at the neighborhood beauty shop at four. There was something so blissfully extravagant about having your hair done at a regular shop, instead of just putting it up in pin curls; and the beauty shop always smelled so luxurious—creams and lotions and nail lacquer.

The house was in shining readiness by the time Jennifer had to leave for her appointment. The juke-box had arrived and was in the corner of the living room, where it had displaced the television set. It looked gaudy and festive with its flickering red and blue and orange and green lights all melting together. Jennifer had plugged it in right away and adjusted the tone so it wouldn't blast them out of the house. There were flowers in all the vases, and the rug had been rolled up and put in the closet. The bare polished floor gleamed, and the lamps were placed strategically to give just the right amount of dreamy light.

"It's going to be a lovely party," Jenny said, for about the twentieth time.

She left her mother icing a regiment of little cakes and flew to keep her date with the hairdresser.

Jennifer came back a scant hour later to find the house strangely silent. "Hi, Mom!" she called. "Where are you?" She didn't wait for an answer but moved quickly from one room to the other. "Hey, Mom! Come look at me. I'm all glamoured up."

She was impatient, but not really alarmed, when she ran next door to ask Mrs. Ferris if her mother was there. "Why, no, dear. I haven't seen her since this morning, when she came over to borrow the candlesticks." Mrs. Ferris's plump face clouded a little at the sudden anxiety in Jennifer's eyes. "Now don't start worrying about her. She might have run down to the corner grocery store."

"I'd have seen her. I was in the beauty shop." Jennifer turned away blindly, but Mrs. Ferris's voice halted her halfway down the walk. "Oh, Jenny! I tried to phone your mother an hour ago, and the operator told me they were holding the line open for a long-distance call."

Jennifer nodded her thanks and ran back to her own house. Everything was in readiness for the party, right down to the candy dishes and the huge platter of rosy apples. She went into her mother's room and looked into the closet. Her mother's coat and hat were missing, her brown gloves and best handbag were gone from the shelf. That certainly ruled out any hurried-trip-to-the-grocery-store theory. She went out on the front porch and looked longingly toward the street, as though her unspoken prayers could somehow conjure up the image of her mother.

A small boy, whizzing past on roller skates, stopped and grinned at her. "Where did your mother go in the taxi?" he demanded.

A taxi!

Jennifer went back into the house and closed the door carefully behind her. The long-distance call and then the taxi! She was sure they fitted together, but how? *How?*

Perhaps one of her mother's old friends had been passing through town. "I'll be at the airport for about an hour, Nan. How about joining me for a quick one? We can hash over old times."

Jennifer sat down on the straight chair in the hall and clasped her hands together. She decided not to call her father. What would be the use? There was no one in this town who could help them locate her mother. It was past six, anyway, and Dad was probably on his way home. In a little while he would walk

in and look around and say, "Where's your mother?"
the way he always did, and she would have to tell him.

"I don't know," she would have to say. "She went
out. She was gone when I got back from the beauty
shop." She wouldn't say, "I knew it couldn't last! I
knew it couldn't! It's starting all over again, just like
all those other times." She wouldn't say anything, she
wouldn't have to.

"I can't bear it." She said the words aloud in the
echoing stillness. "I can't *bear* it."

The telephone rang demandingly and she looked
at it for a while before she reached over and picked
it up. She spoke quietly enough into the mouthpiece,
and her father's voice came rushing over the wire. He
sounded breathless and excited. "Look, Snooks! I got
tied up with an old business associate and it looks as
if I might not be able to break away for a few hours.
I'm sorry, but this is one of those things I couldn't
get out of. I'll tell you about it when I see you." He
broke off and she heard him talking to someone in
a hurried aside before he finished. "Tell Nan I'll see
her about nine-thirty or ten. And don't worry about
getting your guests home. I'll be there in plenty of
time to deliver them around. O.K.?"

"O.K.," she said tonelessly.

"Did the jukebox get there? Is everything rolling?"

"Everything's just fine," she said.

"Well, I suppose you gals have a million things to attend to. Have a good time and be sure to save me a sandwich."

What am I going to do? What am I going to do? Her father would be furious because she hadn't warned him. What if he took this business associate to dinner at some restaurant and Mother happened in and came weaving up to the table? What if. . . .

She pushed the disquieting thoughts aside and got to her feet. It was time to take her bath and start getting ready for the party. She took the telephone clear to the end of its long extension cord and put it just outside the bathroom door so that she wouldn't miss a call.

What am I going to do? What am I going to do? She took as long as she could getting ready, telling herself every moment that her mother would pop into the house at any time with some perfectly logical explanation. She had run in to visit a neighbor. But . . . her good hat and coat and purse and gloves were gone. And what about the taxi . . . what about the long-distance call?

She was dressed at last, ready to go out and wait for her guests. She wore the daffodil-yellow sweater that was her favorite, and a slim brown skirt, and she had a matching brown velvet ribbon tied around her throat. She had brushed and brushed her hair until it glistened, and then pushed it back from the careful curls the beauty operator had arranged so painstakingly.

She had decided exactly what she would say to Patsy when she arrived. Patsy was coming a little before the others to help with the last-minute details. She would say it casually, as if it happened all the time. "Dad has a big account that he has to keep happy. Lots of times he and Mother have to entertain people on the spur of the moment like this. Isn't it lucky that everything is ready?"

And then she would pray that her mother didn't wander in when the party was at its height, with her eyes bright and her speech too carefully modulated and her steps just a little unsteady, like the time. . . .

Jennifer hurried through the hallway and across the gleaming waxed floor to punch a button on the jukebox. Music swelled into the room—a popular dance number that the kids would love.

Patsy came rushing up the walk at the last possible minute. She explained breathlessly that her date would stop by and pick up Ed Winters. "Ed gets off at eight-thirty and Hank said he'd wait for him."

"That's good," Jennifer said. "Since Diane will be coming with Griff. . . ."

Just as if it didn't matter. With a little sense of shock she realized that it *didn't* matter . . . not really. It was something that she might not even remember a year from now—nothing like this fear that crowded her throat and made breathing difficult, this pity that was all mixed up with love and disappointment and shame.

With Patsy she made a hasty last-minute tour of the house, stuffing more Cokes into the refrigerator, placing the candy and nut dishes in strategic spots.

"It's going to be a dreamy party, Jennifer, just dreamy," Patsy bubbled. "And that sweater of yours is just the last word. The absolute *end*."

The others came, by twos and threes and in groups. Diane and Griff were almost the last to arrive, and Jennifer couldn't help wondering whether Diane had been ready and waiting for a long time before Griff called to pick her up.

All the girls clustered in Jennifer's room, dumping their coats on her bed and applying fresh lipstick before her dressing-table mirror. There was a lot of chatter and laughter, and some of the girls looked around with eyes that were frankly envious. "Your room is just darling, Jenny!" "You ought to see my room! It looks like something that should be stuck away in the attic." "Is this hi-fi set yours, Jenny? Do all these record albums belong to you?"

It should have been gay and heart-warming, but somehow it wasn't. Jennifer held her smile steady and traded wisecracks back and forth, but all the time she was braced for the moment when the doorbell might peal, or the telephone ring.

The jukebox was blaring; someone had found the button to turn up the volume. Jennifer turned it down again, explaining that they had to consider the neighbors. Everyone had accepted her explanation without question when she told them about her father's business appointment.

When Hank and Ed arrived, most of the boys were gathered in a neutral corner discussing sports cars. Ed had brought her a present.

Jennifer's eyes widened when he put the clumsily wrapped box into her hands. "But Ed, it isn't a birthday party."

"I know. And it isn't a present for you, really. It's for your tree."

"Our tree?"

"Yes. I heard the kids talking about it one day."

Jennifer was busy opening the package. Her head was tipped forward so that he could just see the flushed curve of her cheek. "I guess it does seem pretty silly—caring so much about a tree."

"It doesn't seem silly to me. There's something so stable about a tree—so permanent. I took special notice of it when we came up the street. I'd like to have a tree like that in my family, too."

Why, he's really nice, Jennifer thought. And of all

the boys and girls she'd met so far he was the only one who understood what she felt about her tree— that it wasn't just showing off and trying to be different, that it wasn't just sentimental.

The present for the tree was a birdhouse, a small perfect replica of a real house—a one-story structure with sketched-in windows and doors and a softly sloping roof. There was a fireplace on one side, and a trellis beside the front door.

Jennifer looked up at Ed with dawning recognition in her grave eyes. "Why, it's *our* house. It's this house, isn't it?"

He gave her a pleased grin. "Glad you recognized it. Yes, that's a hobby of mine. I made several of these for friends of mine when we were in California."

The others gathered around them, admiring the present and wanting to go out and see the tree. Then a new record blared out and they all went back into the living room again.

Jennifer stood in the hallway with the little white house in her hands. Her eyes felt hot and dry as she looked at it—the white house that had held all the hopes and dreams and plans of the three of them. The hopes had looked toward all the tomorrows, the dreams had turned away from all the heartbreaking yesterdays. The plans . . . the lovely plans. . . .

She lifted her eyes to Ed's watchful face and he

frowned a little. "You don't like it," he said flatly.

"I love it," she said. "It's beautiful. But it must have taken you hours and hours."

He shrugged. "I worked on it at the service station, nights when we weren't very busy. It took a couple of weeks, I imagine."

Jennifer started to say that a couple of weeks ago she hadn't even met him. Why had he been making a birdhouse for her, when he hadn't even met her? Her cheeks felt hot all of a sudden, but she spoke in a curiously adult voice. "Thank you, Ed. I know our tree will love her present."

The others had started to dance. Most of the girls had kicked off their shoes. Sock dances were more fun. Patsy was passing around the Cokes and Elsie was serving potato chips. It was all just the way she had planned it, young and hilarious, but her heart was broken.

Ed was watching her soberly. "Grab a coat, why don't you? We'll go out and give the tree her present right now. I put this hook on it so I can anchor it to a branch."

No one even missed them. Jennifer got her coat from the hall closet and they went out of the house and down the walk. Ed swung himself up into the tree and reached down for Jennifer to hand him the little house.

While he was clamping it into place, a taxi careened around the corner and drew to a stop before the house! Jennifer stood very still as the driver got out and ran around to open the door. Her mother paid him and then turned to murmur something to the woman who followed her out of the cab. Jennifer felt frozen to the spot. She couldn't manage to say a word.

Ed swung down from the tree and dusted off his hands and knees. His grin was young and friendly. "Good evening. You must be Jennifer's mother," he said, because Jennifer was still silent. "I'm Ed Winters and I just brought your tree a small present."

Jennifer's mother admired the little house and then led the way to the house. "How's the party going, dear?" she asked. "Is Daddy being a proper chaperon and staying in the kitchen, where he belongs?"

She introduced the woman with her as Mrs. Kopley, and when Mrs. Kopley had left them and gone to remove her coat and hat Jenny and her mother had a few hurried words together in the comparative privacy of the kitchen.

"But darling, didn't you get the message I left at Dad's office? I called and told him to be sure and call you right back, so that you wouldn't worry. And I said he was to hurry home and hold the fort, in case I was later than I expected to be. I left a note for you on the telephone pad, too, but I suppose you never thought to look for it."

"No, I didn't. And Dad didn't get your message either. He's been tied up most of the day with some business associate and he didn't even go back to the office." She swallowed. "Where were you, Mother?"

Her mother glanced at the door and then spoke hurriedly. "Mrs. Kirby called me long-distance about Mrs. Kopley. She really needed help, desperately, so there was nothing to do but drive out there and persuade her to come home with me. I hope you don't mind, Jennifer. It was too bad it had to come at the same time as your party."

"Of course I don't mind."

"Because it's so wonderful to—to be able to offer a helping hand to someone else. There aren't too many of us who . . . understand Mrs. Kopley's problem."

Jenny put her arm around her mother's shoulder and pressed her flushed cheek against her mother's cool one. "I love you, Mom!" she said. "I'm so proud of you!"

"Why, that's nice," her mother said. "Run back to your party now, and have a wonderful time."

"Oh, I will," Jenny assured her fervently. "I'll have an absolute ball."

The rest of the evening passed as if in a dream.

They danced and danced. It seemed almost too much to ask, but Ed Winters turned out to be a beautiful dancer. Not only that—he made no secret of the fact that he preferred Jennifer as a partner.

"In California we had dances at the school every week. If you couldn't dance you were just dead," he explained matter-of-factly. "Anyway, Diane's been practicing on me since I was about twelve." He glanced at his sister, who was sitting on the floor beside the jukebox. "Di's a swell dancer—almost as good as you are, Jenny."

Jennifer glanced at Diane and almost felt sorry for her. In just a little while there'd be a new girl in town, but maybe Diane would be lucky enough to find someone like Ed when that time came.

Jennifer's father came in just as they were eating and she was proud to introduce him to all her friends. When the party broke up he drove some of them home and Jenny went along for the ride.

"Thanks, Jenny! Swell party," they said, as they scrambled out of the car. "Good night, Jenny. Thanks again." And those who remembered their manners said, "Thank you very much, Mr. Martin."

Jennifer and her father drove home and he put the car away. Mrs. Kopley wouldn't let them drive her home. She wanted to go on the bus. "You've gone to enough trouble already for a perfect stranger," she said firmly. "I do appreciate it, but enough is enough."

"But Mother, will she be . . . that is . . . all right?" Jennifer whispered the words while Mrs. Kopley was getting her hat and coat.

Jennifer's mother met her eyes gravely. "I think so, Jenny, but at any rate this is something she has to find out for herself. I'll walk to the bus stop with her."

Jennifer knew that she and her mother were both thinking about the twenty-two days before they had come out to this new place, this new life. The days when her mother had to prove to *herself* that she could be strong and sure.

"I'll walk along with you," Jenny offered. "Then you won't have to walk back alone."

But her mother shook her head. "No, she may want to talk to me, Jenny."

Her father came in and they all said good night to Mrs. Kopley and invited her to visit them again. When the two had gone, Jennifer turned to her father. "Mother wasn't here when I came home from the beauty shop," she said carefully. "I looked in her closet and her good clothes were gone, and Mrs. Ferris said there'd been a long-distance call. Some little boy said he'd seen her driving off in a taxi. I thought . . . well, naturally I thought. . . ." She put her hands up before her face to hide the swift rush of tears and spoke in a muffled voice. "Oh, Dad, I'm so ashamed!"

His arm went around her shoulder and there was comfort and strength in his reply. "I know, sweetie. I know better than you can possibly imagine." He gave her shoulder an awkward little pat. "Come along. I want to show you something."

He led her into the bedroom he and her mother shared, and opened the closet door. A half-filled bottle was stuffed carelessly into his shoe bag.

"It's been there all the time, Jenny. Ever since we first moved here. I hope your mother never suspected how often I've checked, measuring and weighing, just to make sure."

She nodded, and he led her back into the front room and offered her his clean handkerchief so that she could dry her eyes. "Run out and meet her, Jenny. I'll disconnect the jukebox and start picking things up." He looked around the room and shook his head in pretended dismay. "Such a mess!"

Jenny pulled her coat around her and hurried outside. She waited in the friendly shadow of the tree and once she tipped her head back and smiled up at the little birdhouse, remembering Ed's easy smile, the warmth in his eyes and the smooth way he moved around a dance floor.

He hadn't ever had much time for girls, Diane had told Jennifer. "Ed's always had to work so hard. It'll be easier for him now that Mother's getting married again and he doesn't have to worry about being the man of the house."

Jennifer's mother was coming briskly along the street from the bus stop. Her step was light and quick, like the step of a young girl, and she waved when she saw Jennifer standing there waiting.

"Hello, darling. Did you come to meet me?" she said, as soon as she was close enough.

They linked arms and started up the walk together. Jennifer's father was standing in the open doorway.

Jennifer turned her head and looked back at the tree. "Yes, Mother," she said, "and I wanted to take another look at the birdhouse Ed made for our lovely tree."